THE HOLLOW CROWN
The Story of St. Edmund

M. Champion
Cover illustration courtesy of
Trinity College, Cambridge
MS No. R.17.1, fol.283v

First published by
Timescape Publishing
The Thatched Cottage
Manor Farm
Kerdiston
Reepham
Norfolk
NR10 4RY

ISBN 0 9531851 0 9

Typeset in Worcester 10pt solid

Produced and printed in England by
Albion Graphics, Norfolk.

Dedicated to
my father

THE HOLLOW CROWN

For God's sake let us sit upon the ground
And tell sad stories of the death of Kings:
How some have been depos'd, some slain in war,
Some haunted by the ghosts they have depos'd,
Some poisoned by their wives, some sleeping kill'd
All murder'd - for within the hollow crown
That rounds the mortal temples of a king
Keeps death his court.

Rich II, Act 3, Scene 2.

Foreword

To describe this small book as a fiction is, perhaps, to do it an injustice. I cannot, by any stretch of the imagination, call it a history for that implies that most of what is contained between the covers is undeniable truth. The only title possible for such a work as this is a Faction. A blend of fact, fiction and conjecture. The truth is contained within most of the background detail. There was a King Edmund of East Anglia, a Danish invasion and an armour bearer, but beyond that it is difficult to say where the truth ends and the stories begin.

I suppose this has always been the trouble with the whole Edmund story. The truth is contained only in tiny fragments that survived the onslaught of the Danish invaders. Anything else that we add to any of the original source material must be treated with extreme suspicion.

When I first became involved with the story of Edmund I cannot really tell. He has been around all my life. Being born and raised in East Anglia it is difficult to avoid reference to our saintly king and throughout my early life he seemed to be always somewhere in the background. I simply accepted him as just another musty old saint. It was only in my early twenties, when I joined a medieval research society, that I took a greater interest in the origins of, what had by that time become, my favourite saint.

What I discovered was that, when the late medieval tales and romances had been removed from the original stories, very little remained. Suddenly the saint became a man of mystery. I was intrigued. I decided to start my own little investigation. This study took me down many paths, local libraries, secondhand bookshops, museums and even Viking re-enactments. I leafed through catalogues of Anglo-Saxon artefacts, studied period poetry and become something of the local bore when I discussed Anglo-Saxon warfare. Even my accountant now knows more about ninth century East Anglia than is entirely healthy.

Several years have passed since I first sat down to write what I had managed to discover about St. Edmund and the format has changed many times. The format that I finally settled upon- the blending of fictional narrative with long historical footnotes- is, I believe, the most interesting way of presenting what few facts really are known and still making it an interesting read. I have played about with a few of the facts, added sections of informed conjecture and generally taken a few liberties which I am sure would make serious historians cringe; but what I am left with is what I present before you, the reader, with this warning- I could be wrong.

There are many people without whom this book would never have seen the light of day, notably: Chris Mycock, [St Edmundsbury Museums]; Brian Attridge; Chris Copage [Albion Graphics]; A.E. Mason; Philip and Margaret Hollis; Kim Siddorn, [Regia Anglorum]; and Gerry Embleton. Most of all I must thank my wife Rebecca, who has so patiently listened to each section of this work and whose observations added much to its final form.

'So long as I have lived I have striven to live worthily. I desire to leave men who come after me a rememberance of good works' - King Alfred.

Introduction

Just as King Arthur became the human symbol of the early Britons' struggle against the Saxon invaders, so too for the Saxons, King Edmund of East Anglia became the symbol of their fight against the Danes. Legends grew up around both figures as symbols of an early Christian hero fighting against the heathen horde and being willing to die for the sake of Christianity.

The early English Church took Edmund to its bosom as the saint who, refusing to renounce his faith, died with the name of Christ upon his lips.

The Anglo-Saxon Church, knowingly or unknowingly drawing parallels between the crucifixion and the martyrdom of Edmund, created a figure that, to this day, has the ability to unite Christians and divide historians. They began with a king of whom little was known and ended with a legend in which the real man had become unimportant. They had created a symbol of Christian light that shone even as the heathen darkness swept over them.

This saintly king fought a desperate battle, a battle for both his kingdom and his faith, that led to his capture and death. At a time when all of England looked as though it was to be plunged once more into the pagan darkness the Church created a legendary saint for the people to follow.

But, unlike later popular heroes who inspired legends, such as Robin Hood, Jesse James or Bonnie and Clyde, Edmund was not a man of the people, nor a peasant made good against all opposition, but a king. A man who could command the respect of other kings and in turn inspire them to follow his lead and fight to the last under Christ's banner.

Within the lifetime of his own contemporaries the Church had made of Edmund a saint and martyr. Alfred, poet king of Wessex, had begun to turn the tide against the pagan Danes and the Church had been eased of it's fear of destruction and the legend had begun to grow. Stories accumulated around Edmund. His life had already passed from the reality of Anglo-Saxon England into the realms of legend. The facts had blurred and the stories defined themselves until it was the stories alone that were held to be the truth. The stories were retold, generation after generation, until along with King Arthur, Edmund the man had become hidden behind Edmund the saint.

Yet among these legends and stories, created by a needy people, there is a basis of truth. Beyond the miracles and incense of the early mediaeval church it is just possible to glimpse the image of a man. Edmund, Anglo-Saxon king of East Anglia.

The Witness.

The truth. That is a difficult master to follow. Throughout my long life I have followed many masters, some good and some bad, but I have followed and served them as well as I could. This master that is truth is now the hardest of all to follow. It is a master that, although I have lived over seventy years in the world, I have seldom met.

Now I will attempt to tell the truth. I will tell all as I remember it and, unlike Aelfric's polished tales of past glories, I will try and at least keep to the facts. The facts that I know and the facts as my memory shows them to me.

Memory is a strange thing. I lie now in my small room, bitterly feeling the chill draughts, and try to warm myself on memories. They come to me easily, yet it is always the memories of my early days that seem clearest in my head. If I must remember something that happened yesterday then I must play it over and over again through my mind and hope that it lodges somewhere within. If I wish to recall the events of sixty years ago then I need only close my eyes and let my mind drift for a moment. Then I am back among them all. I can find myself bridging the years now with more ease than I can put on my boots.

Memory can play tricks upon an old mind. I will try and remember the truth but if a trick slips through my mind I ask your forgivness. Treat them as the ramblings of an old man and set no store by them. But remember also that somewhere within the tangled web that is all that is left of my mind is the essential truth. The true story of what happened all those years ago.

I do not say that it is the only truth, for each man's truth is different. but it is how I saw it all. How I witnessed the splendour and the horror of that summer long ago. How I carried my lord king's shield into battle against the heathens and how I stood by and watched the death of my beloved lord. It is not his story but mine, and I can only hope that the one can shed light upon the other. Believe what you will but this is my tale.

Contemporary Sources

When approaching a story such as that of St. Edmund the most important thing for any interested party is to remember to keep an open mind. Over the centuries many hundreds of books and articles have been written and a vast web of complex and often contradictory stories have appeared. It becomes obvious to even the most casual observer that not all can be true but it also becomes difficult to try and sieve through the mass to discover where each version has it's origin. Somewhere among the great piles of chaff a grain of truth must rest and this search, rather than the saint himself, becomes the object of the quest. To have any hope at all of rediscovering what remains of the original you must discount all of the later writings and return to the original source material from which they were formed.

Original source material concerning the ninth century kingdom ruled by Edmund is scarce and unlike the kingdom of Wessex, whose history is well documented, little survives concerning East Anglia. It is almost as though the invaders swept away the past, and to some extent, this is true. In their attack on East Anglia the Danes made a point of destroying the monastic settlements and religious houses that the Christian Anglo-Saxons had built to the glory of God. The devotion of the local inhabitants meant that these sites had gained great wealth in the preceding centuries and once the valuables were removed the monasteries were razed to the ground. Unfortunately, for modern historians, the monasteries had also become the regional centres for learning and literacy and so when they were destroyed so too were the written records for the entire kingdom. The subsequent Danish victory over the forces of Edmund ensured that few escaped to carry either written or verbal records with them.

The only original written source material that may be accepted as reliable, at least in part, is the Anglo-Saxon Chronicles. This collection of manuscripts compiled in the ninth century is a history of England and nearby continental Europe from the birth of Christ onwards. Although unreliable in much of its early content it does appear to give a factual account of the events of ninth century England and the events surrounding the Danish invasion of 866. Yet even this near contemporary account has only this to say concerning the death of Edmund and the defeat of the East Anglians:

'The force went over Mercia (from York) to East Anglia and took, winter quarters at Thetford. In that year, St. Edmund the king fought against them atrociter (all out) and the Danes took the victory, killed the king, and overcame all the land. They destroyed all the churches they came to; the same time they came to Peterborough, they burned and broke, killed the Abbot and monks, and.all that they found there. They made that which was very great such that it became nothing.'

The only other source of any real historical value is that written by Abbo of Fleury in about 985. Although written nearly 120 years after the event it has a modest claim at accuracy as Abbo supposedly copied the story down from a tale told by St Dunstan. As a young man St. Dunstan, the story tells, was a member of the party of King Athelstan upon his visit to the shrine at Bury St Edmunds. There the head of the secular canons who tended the shrine produced before the king an eyewitness to the events of 870. An old man was brought forward and it was claimed that as a boy this old man had been armour bearer to Edmund during his fight against the invaders.

The position of armour bearer was a position of honour usually given to young sons of noble families and so it is likely that this eyewitness was of a high ranking Saxon family who would, therefore, have been accepted in good faith.

St Dunstan was impressed with the story of St Edmund and retold it often, until Abbo finally committed it to writing. Unfortunately for modern historians Abbo only began recording the story with the martyrdom and no mention of the preceding campaign is made. This omission on the part of either the armour bearer, St. Dunstan or Abbo of Fleury has meant that for over a millenium historians have had few resources available with which to recreate the events leading up to Edmund's death. It is in Abbo's account that we first come across the name of the site of Edmund's martyrdom. He states that the king died after the battle against the invaders at a place called 'Haegelisdun'.

Although these two sources, the Chronicle and Abbo, are the principal texts upon the events of Edmund's death it is worth mentioning several other texts.

One of the earliest post conquest accounts of the martyrdom of Edmund is that written in about 1098 by Archdeacon Hermann. This is of main interest in the fact that Hermann gives the site of Edmund's original martyrdom and burial the name 'Suthtuna' and rejects Abbo's 'Haegelisdun'. In recent years the name 'Suthtuna' has been suggested to be translatable into Sutton, a not uncommon place name in East Anglia. Hermann claimed that his story was correct as he had it from a very old book that was difficult to read and contained even older stories. This may suggest that Hermann was copying the story from an old Anglo-Saxon manuscript although it is just as possible that he was of Norman descent, as his name suggests, and had difficulty reading the Anglicised latin of pre-conquest England.

One of the texts best known today is that written by Geofrey of Wells, an Augustine canon of Thetford, in about 1150. Geofrey's account chronicles the early life and lineage of Edmund and although he was personal friends with Abbot Ording of Bury it appears to have little factual basis and in structure bears more resemblance to an early medieval romance.

Geofrey of Wells account claims that Edmund was adopted as heir to the East Anglian throne by King Offa (1) and that he was a younger son of a royal house of Saxony. Offa died on pilgrimage to the Holy Land and Edmund was transported as the new king to East Anglia. Geofrey goes on to claim that Edmund was crowned at Bures in Suffolk on Christmas day 855. Of the fourteen years of Edmund's reign between his coronation and martyrdom Geofrey has little to say except that he was 'as firm of purpose as merciful in action'.

It is at this point probably worth mentioning the reasons given by Geofrey for the Danish invasion as, in some form or other, this story has been repeated with slight variations and additions for over 800 years.

Geofrey tells that Lodebrok, an infamous Danish pirate, upbraided his three sons for being lazy and making little of their lives. Pointing to Ednund as an example of how to get on in the world he so enraged his sons that they invaded East Anglia and killed Edmund.

It is from Geofrey of Wells' text that much of what has later been accepted as fact first originates. Very little of his elaborate tale has any factual basis and much of it can be proved to be inaccurate.

The final text is that which has today become known as the 'Bury Tradition' and dates from the time of Abbot Curteys in the early 15th century. This is the final form in which the story of Edmund has survived to the present day, yet little if any of it can be thought of as reliable or factual. It mainly consists of a series of stories relating to the miraculous St Edmund and expands upon the romance of the earlier stories as told by Abbo and Geofrey. Although several of the stories it contains do seem to have a source in antiquity, being written over 500 years after the event, it cannot be thought of as more than an amusing retelling and reshaping of what had by that time become a legend.

One small story related in the Bury Tradition is however worth repeating. It very simply states that after being defeated by the Danes in a battle, Edmund miraculously escaped across a ford at a place called Dernford. What makes this particular story so interesting is the way in which it is merely mentioned in passing with no elaboration or ornamentation and that no such place as Dernford can now be identified. It is also the only story which actually names a specific place which is not a major town or religious site. It is almost as though it was included simply because the basic story was always part of the tradition and yet made little sense to those who were recording it in the later middle ages. It is pleasant to speculate that this may perhaps be part of an earlier factual account.

In recent centuries several accounts and books have been written concerning the life and death of St. Edmund and of these Lord Francis Hervey's 'Corolla, Sancti Edmundi' must be regarded as the first modern attempt to bring together all the earlier material. Published in 1907 it is a collection of the early medieval legends and as Lord Francis seems to have virtually ignored the earlier Anglo-Saxon Chronicles there is little in it of any historical interest. In 1932 the 'Harvard studies and notes in Philology and Literature' published an article by Grant Loomis in which he analizes the legends collected by Lord Francis and estimated that a 'veritable saga' had collected around a 'mere scrap of history'.

It is only in writings that have appeared in the last century that any real arguments have begun to appear around the whole Edmund story. The main point of contention in all recent waiting has been the exact whereabouts of the site of Edmund's martyrdom. This debate has been fuelled by publication after publication each putting forward theories of their own.

Of the accounts written in the last half century Bryan Houghton's 'St Edmund, King and Martyr' is probably the most widely read. Most later writings are merely retellings of the later stories surrounding Edmund and contain little that sheds any greater light upon the original sources. In many cases they have succeeded only in adding to the confusion. Like Bryan Houghton's work, most have been written from a religious perspective with scant attention paid to the historical background.

Houghton even goes as far as to discuss a resistance war fought by Edmund against the Danes when they first landed in 865, a fact flatly contradicted by the only contemporary source available. In the Anglo-Saxon Chronicle it clearly states that the East Anglians made peace with the invaders. Houghton goes on to state that the Danes used cavalry when all sources from the period state that the Danes fought on foot and only used horses for transport. Apart from these obvious historical blunders Houghton seems more interested in discovering the modern resting place of the relics of St Edmund.

Since Houghton's publication in 1970 every other work seems in contrast to have concentrated upon the argument as to whether Edmund was martyred at Hoxne or Hellesdon both of which are considered to be modern adaptations of Abbo of Fleury's 'Heagelisdun'.

For the purpose of this study original sources have been used wherever possible and every attempt has been made to discount anything written after the Bury tradition as committed to paper by Abbot Curteys in the fifteenth century.

The Witness

The day has been a long one and now I am tired. The wind has a bitter edge to it and it makes me afraid that the spring will never come again. These cruel, dark days are hard on the body of an old man and I am older than most here. Even the older monks show me some respect for my years. The younger ones merely snigger behind my back.

I have returned to my bed early today and now lie, swathed in rough blankets, and try to will warmth back into my old bones.

Bones. Bones are the reason I am here. I, who was once a proud warrior who fought the heathens through many summer campaigns, am now a mere curiosity attached to a coffin of old bones. It is not even my bones that are important though they still have flesh sparingly covering them. It is the bones in the casket that they all adore. They venerate the dead, lifeless sticks and ignore the bones I drag past them each day.

Yet I should not be unkind to them. They treat me well. They feed me and clothe me and unlike them I have a private cell to myself. I am well looked after in my dying years. For dying I am.

Soon I'll join the man whose bones they love so dearly. Soon I'll walk again with my king in the land they call the summer country. But then these bones of mine may find rest. Not like the others, swathed in silk and laid in a silver faced coffin on the high altar, but among the bones of those who have gone before in the churche's graveyard. A deep and peaceful sleep, undisturbed by the prying eyes of the inquisitive monks. A better resting place by far than that of my namesake.

Today has taken its toll on me and left my throat dry and my legs aching but I have paid my dues, once again, to those who care for my bodily needs. I have retold my story. The story of my youth and of the summer of madness. The story of their St. Edmund. My king Edmund.

Today I told my story to another king. He came here yesterday with his fine horses and proud looking men to pray at the shrine of my king. As is usual upon these occasions they ate well, slept little and prayed even less. The whole house was in disorder and as I lie here in my peaceful solitude I can feel the rhythm of the days trying to reassert itself. It will be a week or so before all is back to normal, and a week after that before the younger monks return to their normal selfish selves. So perhaps I have a couple of weeks in which they may treat me well and show me the respect my years deserve.

It is ever so after the visit of a lord or bishop to our church. I am called to tell my tale, I become the centre of all attention, I hold the place of honour and for a week or so afterwards am treated with an almost holy reverence. Then, when I stumble in the cloister or fall asleep in the church I am seen for nothing more than the ancient that I am and all is returned to normal. Perhaps this time it will be different. It is not every day that a king visits our humble house.

9

He seemed like a good man, this king who came. He listened to my story not just for the sake of his soul but because he enjoyed the story. I could tell. He is one of the old sort. A king who fights and likes to hear stories of other fights. My king, who lies cold coffined in the church, was a fighting king. This king Athelstan enjoyed the story and I am sure would have asked me to tell more of the early years had it not been for the monk.

The monk never left his side for a moment, always leaning over his shoulder, whispering into his ear. A long lanky fellow who smelt of chicken fat and had the pale face of a cloister rat. I could tell from the moment he saw me that he disliked me. Who can blame him? I am not a pretty sight these days, my arm hanging limp at my side and half my face refusing to move. I can't be much for a man to look at.

Well, if the monk disliked me I can truthfully say I hold no love for him. In my day a king was guided by warriors and nobles not a lily face streak of piss like him. If he had been at Edmund's hearth he would have had little ease and soon be parcelled off with the women. At least there he could have made himself useful. Giving beauty tips no doubt.

Well now, he and the king are gone and I am alone in my cell. Alone with my memories. My memories and the cold.

In my youth I never remember feeling the cold. I was always warm. Winters were kinder and the summers longer and I would never take to my bed before the last light had drained from the sky. But perhaps these things are merely the tricks that time plays on an old man's memory. Now I am old all I have left are my memories. Cruel fate to play tricks on the one thing an old man has left. Yet I still remember it all so clearly.

It rings through my mind as clear as the bells from our own church and at night they all come back to me and whisper their stories in my mind. Each day I awake and still they are with me. The ghosts of those that have gone before. They hide in the corner of my cell, in the shadows of the church, in the candle flames on the altar. All I have to do is to let my mind wander free and they are with me again, telling me their stories. The story of my youth. The story of Edmund and the summer of madness.

I was born in my father's manor near the coast in the year that Edmund became king of the eastern lands. It was at the beginning of winter and my father was away to the south by the river Stour, the southernmost border of the kingdom, to witness the oath swearing of the new king. My mother and her bond women had been left at the manor by the sea in the hope that it would be a warmer place for her confinement. The winds from the ocean would keep the ice from the doors and make life a little easier for all around the household. I think my father also felt it would be safer to be on our secluded manor. We also owned a hall in the city but if there was going to be trouble with the new kings oathswearing then my father thought we should be as far away as possible. My mother nagged him for worrying overmuch. My mother, I was told, was a strong willed woman and took this, her third pregnancy, in her stride. My father always said she was too strong willed, usually with a slight smile on his face, and this was proved to be the case.

The day before the winter feast, a week after my father rode out with his men, my mother went to collect water from the well by the gate. One of her bond women, a fat lump called Agatha who later became my nurse, had a cold and my mother determined that she should stay inside and away from the wind. My mother collected the water but on her return slipped or tripped, it was never made clear, and fell heavily. She was helped back to the warmth of the hall but by then events were overtaking her. The fall must have upset her more than she realized for that evening she went into labour and I was born at about cockcrow the next morning. All around her took this to be a good sign. To have a son born on the winter feast on the day a new king was crowned, even though I was a month early and scrawny, was considered to be a great sign for my future. In honour of the occasion I was given the name of the new king. Edmund.

My father returned four days later. The frosts had hardened the muddy tracks and he and his men made good time. When he arrived he found my mother up giving orders to the farmhands, berating her tirewomen and cursing me for having such a lusty pair of lungs. All his efforts to get my mother to rest were of little use and she claimed that she could easily run a manor and give birth while he was drinking himself stupid with the young king. My father laughed at her and went to play with his new son.

These are of course just the stories told to me of my birth. I could not tell you what truth lies where, but I know one thing about my early years and that is that my father and mother deeply loved each other. I have no really early memories of our household. In fact I do not remember anything before I was five or six summers but what I do remember is a feeling of love and happiness throughout the household. There were no monsters to grip my childhood mind and lodge within. It gives me only a warm feeling when I think of my early years. A feeling like being wrapped in sheepskins in front of a warm fire. No monsters.

My early years were spent either on our manor on the coast or in the city at what father called his great hall. By today's standards it was little more than an overly large barn and outbuildings. It was always crowded with people and the yard was always muddy except in the warmest of summers when the smell of the tanneries outside the stockade permeated everything. I disliked the city and found it crowded with too many restrictions for a growing boy. I do not suppose it was so, and I probably had a very loose rein compared to the young boys taken into the order with the monks today but I was used to the freedom of our country manor where I am sure I ran almost wild.

It was here that I really remember growing up. It was a paradise for a child and all my memories are interspersed with the image of Agatha's sweaty red face puffing along to keep up with her charges. My nurse was probably an angel by most standards and much more tolerant than I deserved. She was always in the background and, whether it was her overweight body or a natural laziness, she always let me do much as I wished. On the few occasions she got me under control I resented it bitterly and as I grew she became the butt of all the cruel and vengeful spite that small boys are capable of. She suffered much at my

small hands and for that I am now truly sorry. She is one of the ghosts that
My mother was probably the greatest influence on my young life, although I saw
little of her. She was ever about the manor keeping a careful eye upon the
running of the household and it was into Agatha's care I was placed for much of
the time. When I did see my mother she was all I could wish for and more
besides. Possibly it was guilt at spending so little time with me, but when we
were together it was possible to believe that I was the new king. To be blunt, and
now in old age I can see it clearly, she spoilt me. If it was in her power to give it
to me, however silly a whim, I got it. This of course only intensified my
resentment at the few mild restraints placed upon me by Agatha.

I am sure now that she knew my true nature but whenever I had done
something particularly irksome, and Agatha drew her attention to it, she was
more likely to reproach my nurse than myself. This can have done little to
recommend me to any of the servants about the manor. In short I now see that I
was a thoroughly spoilt, wilful and vindictive child.

In my early years I remember very little of my father. It seemed to me that he was
ever away at some council meeting or south of the Stour busy selling our wool
fleeces. He was a distant character and I went in some awe of him. He was a
powerful man in the King's hearth guard and led several of the local law courts.
His belief in justice spread to cover all people, even those within his own
household, and I soon found it prudent to curb my temper and be on my best
behaviour when I heard that he was to return from a trip. I had learnt quickly
that he would not be so hasty when taking sides between Agatha and myself,
and it was as often as not I who received the clout round the head that signalled
the end of a dispute.

This, I think, in no way lessened my respect and affection that I had for him. If
anything it probably heightened it and when he was at home I made every effort
to keep in his company. This required a great deal of patience as he would often
sit within the hall for many hours discussing matters of concern or suits of law
with the many local people who sought his council. My father tolerated my
presence readily enough and I suspect that he even thought that my interest was
with the arguments rather than with himself. It was not for him to know that as
like as not I was daydreaming the whole time the discussions went on. I even
perfected the art of dozing while I leant against the warm timbers of the hall
walls. I learnt very little of the art of argument.

In fact, by today's standards, I learnt very little in our manor by the sea. Oh, I
learnt all the usual arts of the country boy, how to snare birds, where the best
fish swam and which of the old folk were too blind to spot a small thief in the
fruit bushes, but little of education passed into my thick arrogant skull. I suspect
that if it had not been for the weary patience of Agatha, and a wandering
holyman my father employed one winter, I would now be as ignorant as any
farm boy. As it is I can reckon well enough and know my letters to have a
passable, if faltering, hand. It was not as though I was stupid, I can recognise
that now, but I was lazy and spoilt. If I wanted to learn something then it
usually came easily to me but I would much rather be off on the beach with the
other children than studying in the gloomy hut that was Agatha's home. I would

far rather be outside doing any task than within. An irony now that I look at myself and realise that my happiest place these long days is within a warm room with a good fire.

I make myself out to seem a very demon, and I suppose to many of the household servants this would have appeared the case, but I could make myself charming enough when the need arose. There were a few on the manor I took time enough to be civil to. Some, it must be said, because they were not averse to giving me a cuff on the ear when I deserved it, but others because I genuinely liked them and wanted their acceptance. With the exception of my father, only one other man stood out above all others in the manor, an old soldier named Aelfric.

I knew little of Aelfric's past except that he had been a soldier and overseer for my father's father. Now, in his old age, my father kept him about to do simple tasks and help out where he could. This arrangement must have suited them both for I knew my father liked the man and I also knew that Aelfric did as little as possible around the manor and farms. Like as not he could be found sitting with his back to the stockade watching the sea and sand. The fact that my father so obviously respected this old soldier made me want to be accepted by him also. Perhaps I thought of it as another way to get close to my father. To be liked by one who he cared so much for would surely place me higher in his estimation. Who knows how the mind of a child works.

Whatever the reasons, I determined that Aelfric should like me. This task of ingratiating myself with the old man proved not as easy as I had suspected. By this time I was some nine or ten years old, and as far as the servants were concerned at my most truculent age. I reasoned that as Aelfric was so apart from the household, often eating alone and never socialising, that I would be as much a mystery to him as he was to me. In this I was sadly mistaken. Although Aelfric seemed never to be about the yard, or involved in the gossip of the servants, he somehow managed to know all that went on in the manor. My reputation had gone before me. As a child I found Aelfric's intimate knowledge of all that went on in the area almost magical. I came to believe that he must have the most acute hearing and could listen to any conversation taking place within half a mile. I now realise that he obviously talked to the other servants at some length but only late in the evening when I was asleep. To me this knowledge of all things around him only added to his attraction and my determination that he should like me increased.

The task of getting Aelfric to like me took much longer than I had hoped. I tried talking to him but received only terse, almost hostile, replies to the questions I bombarded him with. I tried giving him small gifts, choice cuts of meat or apples stolen from the loft, and these he accepted readily enough but they did not bring forth the warmth I had anticipated. Now I can look back and see how he must have been laughing at my attempts. I must have made a strange sight, the lord's son doggedly following the old man wherever he went. What finally cracked his cool shield I cannot say. Perhaps it was my determination or perhaps he just got so used to my being there that I was accepted as always having been there. Whatever the true reason, one day Aelfric just started to talk to me as an equal.

It was a warm day in the late autumn before my tenth birthday and Aelfric had decided it would be a good time to collect the last of the hedge fruit from the bushes in the local woodland. He had taken a willow basket and cloth and left the manor early. I was outside the stockade wandering around in a vague fashion and trying to avoid Agatha when I saw him heading south to the woods on the rise above the manor. By this time I had become a little weary of my attack on his privacy and almost despaired of ever gaining his friendship but I quickly decided to catch him up and join in his hunt. Whether it was the prospect of his company for a whole day or whether it was the thought of the fruit that drove me I do not know, but I soon caught him up and fell into step beside him. We had to walk several miles that day, as all the nearby bushes had been well and truly stripped of their fruit, and throughout the walk neither of us spoke a word.

It was the type of day one only gets in the late Autumn. The sun was still warm but I could feel the chill of winter drawing closer by the day. The distance was blurred by a slight misty haze and the dew lingered long on the ground covering the first of the fallen leaves. We climbed the rise and decended into the next slight valley all the time keeping an eye open for ripe fruit. Aelfric knew where we were going and we soon came to a an area thick with blackberry bushes. Here he stopped and put down the basket. Then he took a cloth and tucked one side into the belt of his tunic and held the further side leaving one hand free to pick the glowing purple fruit. Still no word had been spoken.

I now began to feel like a fool. What was I to do. I could not very well pick a handful of blackberries and then return to the basket. I would be going back and forth all day. Why had I been so stupid as to follow the old man when he obviously wanted nothing to do with me. Sick with despair and helpless anger I felt close to the edge of tears. It was then I noticed the second smaller cloth in the basket.

So suddenly did the truth strike me that I almost did burst into tears. Aelfric had been expecting me to follow him. Had even wanted me to come along. Suddenly the bond was there, if only on my part. From that moment I would have followed that old man anywhere he led.

I took the second cloth and, doing as Aelfric had done, started to fill it with the ripe fruit. We worked together thus for perhaps half an hour occasionally returning to the big basket to empty our precious loads before it happened. Suddenly Aelfric started talking. Not to me you understand, but just talking in general. I was so startled that I dropped the edge of the cloth I was holding and blackberries scattered in all directions. As I scrabbled about the leaf strewn floor retrieving my prizes, Aelfric continued on seeming not to notice my accident. He was telling me a story. A story of his youth, when he had been a soldier under the great king of the eastern lands.

I do not remember exactly what the story was but it held me spellbound. We worked side by side and the story spun its silvery thread around us both. Occasionally I would interject with a question that would be answered before the main thread of the tale progressed but mostly I was silent, sucking in the drama of it all. By the time the tale was ended the basket was full and we returned to the stockade in a companionable silence so different from the silence we had left in.

That tale was the first of many such stories that Aelfric wove for me and always I would draw in every detail, extract every drop of drama and suspense, and savour the feel of each new chapter. For chapters they were. Aelfric was telling to me the tale of our kingdom, showing me its history and leaving me to draw my own morals. Whether he was telling the tales for my sake or for his I was never clear, but I believe that he could see something of what the future had in store for us all and wished to pass on what he knew of our past in the hope that it might be of some use. He was strange that way. Always staring out across the bright ocean but never really seeing it. Whether he was looking backwards or forwards I could never fathom but always somewhere in his tales he talked of the

In the spring after my tenth birthday the threat of the future became a reality.

It had been a hard but short winter and as far as I was concerned more irksome than most. My father had been called away to the Kings council shortly after the winter festival and was away for almost a month. This had left the household, especially Agatha, in a distracted state. It was unusual for a council to be called at such a time and my father had left with a worried look on his face and most of his warriors at his back. It was this last fact that so distressed Agatha as she had finally found herself a man. He was a tall raw boned Dane who had come into my father's guard only the previous autumn and taken an immediate liking to Agatha. He was a solid warrior, so my father said, and obviously liked his women well fleshed. I had liked him well enough when he first arrived and this feeling was expanding rapidly as I saw the effect he was having on my nurse.

So smitten were they both that I spent most of the autumn doing much as I liked while they mooned at each other across the hall. I did not admire his taste but I respected his courage.

It was probably the best time of my young life. I spent most days with Aelfric, listening to his tales and questioning him closely about his warrior past. What little schooling I normally had went by the board and if my mother noticed she forbade to comment. I think she was as amazed as everyone else by the love match that had appeared under her nose. She even got one of the farm's bondmen to leave the harvest and repair Agatha's hut in the obvious hope that it would soon contain two bodies.

So when my father was called away and took Agatha's Dane with him it went hard on all of us. When the snows left early in the new year and the weather turned mild I took to spending a lot of time outside. The spring had come very early and by March the new leaves were already beginning to show on some of the early trees. A sure sign of a bad harvest the old people said for the frosts were bound to return before long and set back any early growth.

I cared little for the farmers' talk for by this time I was back with my adored Aelfric and his tales of past glories. The frosts did return and the harvest was bad that year but by that time we had greater things to trouble ourselves with.

The first we knew of any danger was at the end of March. A horseman rode in at our gate late in the evening and demanded to see my father. I was crossing the yard on the way to my bed at the time so I got a good look at him. He was not a

15

local man and had obviously travelled far and fast by the state of his gear. As his horse stood sweaty and shaking, the man was quickly led into the glowing interior of the timber hall. I followed quickly behind him and slipped into the shadows behind one of the great wooden roof supports lest I should be noticed and sent to my bed. It had been a quiet day with Aelfric away seeing to the first of the lambs being born in the sheepfolds and I did not want to miss any excitement that now presented itself.

From my place of concealment I could make out little more of the man than I had first seen in the darkened yard. His back was to me and I dared not move further forward lest I betrayed my presence. The stranger stood by the central fire and impatiently moved his weight from one foot to the other as he waited for my father to arrive. My father had spent much of the day in the saddle inspecting his various holdings and had arrived home only shortly before the arrival of the stranger. As he emerged from behind the wooden screen that partitioned the family's part of the hall from the main area I saw that lines of worry were deeply etched in his brow. He had changed his tunic but the unexpected arrival had caught him by suprise and he still wore the same mud splattered leggings he had arrived home in.

My father obviously knew the stranger well and greeted him warmly calling for our steward to fetch bread and ale. They then both moved behind the screen, my father drawing the other man gently, but firmly, by the arm. This was a meeting of some importance and privacy for I realized I had never before seen my father take a guest into our family apartments. They were followed some few moments later by the steward and as he disappeared from view I made my move.

Keeping as close as I could to the outside wall, and moving at a crouching run, I made my way to the junction of the timber partition. I had often hidden myself in this secure corner and knew that I was obscured from the view of the rest of the hall by the tables stacked against the thin partition. Several of the house dogs also knew this spot as a warm concealed sanctuary and I had to gently push aside warm muzzles before I could get my ear next to the rough timbers of the partition.

As is the way with such things I expected much more than I received. Instead of being able to make out the conversation and spy upon my father and his guest I could hear little more than a dull murmuring. Pressing my ear ever closer to the boards and holding my breath seemed to help the situation but little. I managed to make out but the odd word, and those of no consequence, and in return for this small gain impaled my earlobe upon a sharp splinter.

The interview was soon over and as the stranger and my father re-emerged into the hall I ducked down to bury myself among the soft warmth of the dogs. The hounds made little remark upon this and it being late I soon added my own small snores to those of the pack that surrounded me.

I would have stayed thus all night, slumbering with the dogs, if the stacked tables had not been needed. The men who dragged the tables clear disturbed us sleepers and I awoke to find several people bending low over me and passing what they took for amusing comments. As all children are when overtired and suddenly dragged awake I was in a foul mood. I lashed out with my foot and managed to give one of the sleep-blurred images a sharp crack on the shin. As my eyes cleared I soon came to regret my actions. My blow had landed on one of our outdoor workers, a surly fellow who disliked me and was not averse to throwing a slap in my direction for the sheer pleasure of it. I scrambled to my feet and prepared to scream for my mother if he laid so much as a finger on me. I was really a vile young creature.

Much to my surprise all I received in payment for my blow was a cross look and some muttered curses. The men continued to drag the tables and benches into the centre of the hall and when my senses had cleared enough to take in all around me I realized that virtually the entire household was present. Many, bleary eyed like myself, looked as though they too had been raised from their slumber yet there was suprisingly little noise or complaint in the now stuffy hall. All knew that if my father had called together the entire household at this time of night then the matter was not just urgent but of great importance. Worried faces spread around the benches and darting glances were made in my fathers direction. As the last menfolk from the village drifted into the rear of the hall my father came and stood in the centre of the circle made by the crowd. There must have been near forty people crammed into the hall that night and now all their eyes were fixed upon the figure of my father.

I was never more proud of my father than at that moment. All those faces turned towards him, waiting for him to make known his wishes. They each and every one of them looked to my father to be their guide, their leader. A great surge of pride swelled up in my small body and I watched him through eyes misted by tears of pure joy.

He turned in a full circle before he spoke, as though he wished to search every face and reassure the weakhearted. Then out it came, all in a rush. At first I could not believe what he was saying. My ears heard the words yet my head and heart did not take them in. The Danes had landed. They had brought ships into the many inlets to the south of us and landed a great force upon our shore. Several villages had already been burnt to the ground and the king was now calling all armed men to his side. This was no raiding party out for plunder but an army large enough to face down a kingdom.

Shock showed itself all around the hall. In the far corner the little children began to wail, their cries cut short by worried parents, and all faces showed a stunned disbelief. We expected the odd group of raiders to fall upon our shores during the summer months and burn a few remote holdings. It would be an unusual year if they did not come in some shape or form, but this, this was something new to us all. For a force to land in such numbers so early in the year could mean only one thing, an invasion.

My father stood calmly in the centre of the hall issuing orders and suddenly where all had been still silence now a great wave of activity broke out. Orders flooded over us all and people began to rush about to do my father's bidding. Food must be prepared for twenty men. Horses and fodder must be brought into the stockyard. Beacon fires must be made and a watch set on the headland above the village. His voice rang out clearly through the bustle as he gave a list of tasks to be completed by the morning. It was then that he and his followers would ride out to join our king.

I did little to help that night. I tried to lend a hand wherever I could but I seemed to be moving in a daze and the men soon became tired of my sluggish movements and I was packed off to my bed in our private chamber. I slept but fitfully, the quiet movement and continual subdued buzz permeated the very timbers of the hall, and I spent a restless few hours under my heavy blankets. At first light I awoke from a dream ridden sleep to find that the preparations had now spread to my side of the screen. In the dim light cast through the newly opened shutters I could just make out the shadowy figure of my mother. She was near the opposite wall and was kneeling over my father's large wooden clothes chest. Slowly she selected various items of his wardrobe and laid them on a cloth that would then be rolled and attached to his horse. She took great care in her selection, holding each garment up for inspection, rejecting some and passing only a few of his best garments. She seemed to take forever to make up her mind until finally her chosen items were rolled together, but not before she had placed a small bag of coins within the very centre.

As I look back now I can still see that scene as clearly, if not clearer, than I see things today. Now I can truly understand what my mother was feeling. Her slowness perhaps just her way of delaying the inevitable moment when my father would leave her. Now I can feel for her and sympathize with her in a way that was well beyond me in my youth.

I crept out of the hall into the bleached early morning light that was beginning to flood the stock yard and examined all that had gone on in the hours of darkness. The yard was now full of animals. Not only were the horses that my father's troop were to ride present but someone, my father probably, had had the presence of mind to have all our other livestock brought into the shelter of the stockade. Only the sheep were missing, being too far away and already busy with their new lambs. Between the various groups of corraled animals lay the arms and baggage of the soldiers. Dark bundles showing only shiny spines of steel where a sax or sword poked from the cloth.

The yard quickly filled with people. My father was one of the last. He came from the stable building carrying a bundle of rope which he simply shrugged off his shoulder and let drop on a pile of harness. The packs were being quickly hauled onto the waiting horses and made fast with thongs. All around was activity.

My father, in his usual brusque manner, kissed my mother lightly on the lips and said his private farewells into her ear. She blushed slightly, I remember, reluctant to show affection in so public a place. Then my father was striding towards me, a great dark grim figure, all dressed out for war. His farewell to me was simple and yet full of meaning. One hand clasping my shoulder, he looked down into my tired and drawn face and said simply "Take care, take care of all of them."

Within a moment he was gone. I had no time to say even the briefest word before he led his little band of armed men out of the stockade and onto the track that led to the west.

We watched them until they passed from view over the slight rise that cut our manor off from the rest of the world. No words were spoken and after the last horseman had crossed the ridge we all turned, almost as one, and returned to our everyday tasks. Reserved, strained and above all quietly we all tried to make what we could of the new day.

It was not until near midday that the thought struck me. I had been busy through the previous night and the morning that followed but now was at my leisure. My first thought was to go and sit with old Aelfric. I went to find him but he was nowhere to be seen. It was only then I realised I had not seen him the previous night either and that he must still be away with the sheep. No one had remembered he was gone and now, as he sat guarding over our sheep, he was unaware of all that had passed. I determined that he should be informed as soon as possible and after telling a somewhat distracted Agatha of my plans I set out clutching a chunk of bread and a sliver of honeycomb.

Whether I thought that Aelfric should be informed because he would now be of more use back at the manor or whether I just wanted the comfort of his company in these strange times I do not know. Thinking back now, I can see that Agatha for all her distracted manner thought I was in need of comfort for a slice from the precious honeycomb was a rare treat usually reserved for when I was laid low with some childhood ailment.

It took some hours to reach the sheep pens and what with that and the lack of sleep I was near exhausted by the time Aelfric's sturdy frame hove into view. I repeated the events of the previous night to him in a great garbled rush and much to my suprise he merely laughed out loud. Then he sat me down quietly on his old sheepskin cote, for the ground was damp from a light shower, and told me to tell him all again. This time I told the story somewhat slower, giving the details I could remember, and he would ask questions. When I had finished my story I realised that I was calmer than I had been all day. Now Aelfric knew everything it seemed less worrying, somehow less dramatic. Aelfric packed his small bag of belongings that were stored in the sheep hut and we set off once more for our manor by the sea.

The next five days have a slightly disjointed feel to them, at least as far as my memory goes. Aelfric's return could not have come at a better time. We arrived at the manor just before dusk to find all in a state of uproar. One of the boys posted as lookout on the ridge had said that he had seen a ship moving along the coast toward us. By his account this ship was a great dragonship, full to the brim with Danish pirates, and seeking all our blood. This had immediately set off all those poor souls who were nervous enough as it was. It was only careful questioning by Aelfric that brought forth the true story from the boy. A great dragonship soon shrank in size to a small coastal trader heading north out of harm's way.

Over the next five days Aelfric assumed a new stature around the holding. His experience of warfare and level head in times of crisis came to be the stable pillar against which all else was secured. My mother especially came to look to him for guidance in matters that concerned the security of her people. Should the animals, now crowding out the stockyard, be put out to the pasture? Should we send men to the weekly market? Would the market take place?

It had been many years since our eastern land had been involved in a war and my mother had been naught but a girl at the time. She was as nervous as the rest of the household but, because of her station, could not afford to let it show. It was only to the aged Aelfric that she could talk of her worries.

I think that it was at this time that I first started to really grow up. I am sure that my close attachment to Aelfric caused some of his confidence and cool-headedness to pass on to me. I even found some of the women turning to me for answers when Aelfric or my mother were not to be found. This new found responsibility suited my nature well and I stepped into it as one steps into a pair of comfortable boots. Even Agatha started to treat me with a wary respect, half expecting the return of the spoilt brat at any moment.

The days passed in a distant blur. The manor was short-handed and there was much to do. I remember only a few details clearly and the rest is as if I look at it through a spring fog. We went to church on the Sunday, that I do remember. The whole household, save two farmboys, tramped the mile or so down to the small wooden church in the village and I remember my surprise at seeing the great crowd surrounding the small structure. Aelfric merely let out a short derisive laugh. In more normal times the church was sadly neglected during lambing.

In the late afternoon of the fifth day one of the lookout boys came running into the yard shouting that there was an armed horseman approaching from the south. Suddenly all was commotion. Men ran for spears and women ushered their little children inside the hall. Was this a scout for a larger raiding party? The Danish army lay to the south, it was where we had set most of our lookouts. Our fears were soon dispelled as within a few minutes we witnessed Agatha's Danish lover riding in at the gate.

My mother took him into the hall and through to our private chamber, much as my father had done with the previous messenger. This time though she summoned Aelfric to accompany them. I tagged along at Aelfric's heels and to my surprise was not ejected from the meeting. The Dane had come directly from the camp of King Edmund's army. They now lay camped some twenty miles to the south and had raised a passable army with which to face the invaders. They were still outnumbered but it seemed to Edmund that the Danes were not keen for a fight and messengers had been exchanged. My father had sent his man to us to reassure my mother and explain that a fight was now unlikely. Edmund would most probably let the invaders travel across his kingdom unmolested.

Aelfric questioned the Dane closely. Where was the army headed? How many did they number? The Dane answered readily enough, automatically accepting the old warrior's authority. The army, he said, was heading to the northlands where they already had a claim by blood to the land. They had over forty ships' companies with them but had landed farther to the south than expected.

With the spring storms blowing erratically they had taken to the shelter of the nearest rivermouth and dared not travel up the coastline in such heavily laden ships. They intended to march across country with most of their warriors and let the fleet shadow them on the coast.

This seemed to satisfy both Aelfric and my mother for they dismissed the Dane who, no doubt, went to give his greetings to my nurse. I was not so easily satisfied.

For the previous year I had been fed on a diet of Aelfric's stories of past glories and great battles. A rich diet for a young boy and I now found it hard to believe that there was going to be no battle. How could we simply let this army land on our shore and then let it walk away without a scratch? It shocked my young mind that a supposed great king, whom my father served and respected, would trade with an invader rather than fight it. It took a good deal of talk from both Aelfric and the Dane to persuade me otherwise.

They sat me down at the central hearth that night, one on either side and explained to me how they saw what was going on to the south. The very fact that they took so much trouble with me shows how much my distress must have shown to those around me. They explained that we were ill prepared to fight, we had had no warning. It would take more than a single week for Edmund to gather his army. He had only the hard core of his force together in his camp, enough to hold the invaders at bay for a short time in the marshes, but not enough to defeat them. The Danes would have more ships on the way with fresh troops, troops that could land anywhere upon our coast, and we had not the warriors to defend such a great area. Our time would come and if we made a little profit in the meantime then all the better.

This must have had the desired effect upon me for the next few days involved a gradual return to normality around the manor. We were still short-handed so I was given more than my usual amount of work to do about the place but still, whenever I could escape for an hour, I would seek out Aelfric and we would talk of the troubles. We fixed a wary eye to the south and kept the farmboys on lookout, although reduced in number, and this is how I came to be sent off to the sheep folds.

The sheep were lambing in greater numbers now and my father's great flocks were the backbone of his modest fortune so they could not afford to be overlooked. When Aelfric was ready to return to the gentle hills just inland from the coast I asked if I could join him for a few days. He was already taking one of the older lads from the village but an extra pair of hands would come in useful. My mother raised no objection and Agatha was more than happy to be eased of her duties to spend a few peaceful days with her lover. So it was that the three of us set off just before dawn some ten days after my father had left the manor.

I pondered on this fact as we climbed the gentle slope out of our little valley. It seemed so much longer than ten days. It was almost a lifetime to look back upon, so much had happened in such a short space of time. So much had happened to me.

The first grey light was begining to fill the horizon as we crested our little hill and I took a moment to look back down on our manor. Lying in the hollow, still covered with shadows, I could see little more than a darker outline showing where the stockade ran. The hall was merely a dark lumpen shape with a bright rectangle showing where the doors had been opened to let in the chill morning air. As I set off on my first true job of work I looked at all that lay below me and thought of how it had all changed in the previous week. For all of us things would never be the same again.

The days I spent at the sheep pens with Aelfric were, I remember, a happy time. The older lad, a slow but likeable enough fellow, was sent a mile or so further on to keep an eye on another flock and that left Aelfric and me alone for much of the time. We did have some visitors from the local holdings out in search of news or just a gossip but for the most part we were alone. This suited me well for it gave me time to pick the brains of the old soldier. I was still wound up in all the events of the previous days and wanted to hear more of Aelfric's stories. In this he humoured me.

We would sit for hours at a time staring out at the sheep and talking of old campaigns. Lambing is a long tedious task that involves much watching and waiting but we passed the time well enough. Aelfric talking and me, half buried under an old sheepskin, drinking in his words. I wonder now whether he even noticed I was there. I keep it fresh in my memory even today, staring up at his rough profile, while his eyes never left the far horizon. A horizon that, I suspect, he was not really seeing.

It was at that horizon that he was staring, on the third morning of our stay with the sheep, when we realised something was not as it should be. We were expecting someone to come from the manor to bring us food and drink, for our supplies were low, but they were late. It was already mid morning and no figure had yet appeared in the distance. Aelfric was uneasy, I could tell from his general behaviour, he felt that something was wrong. Normally a placid character who could sit for hours moving but little, that morning he could not settle to anything. He stode round the hut, moving something here or mending something there, never settling to any one thing, and always his gaze would return to the horizon.

At about midday he had had enough. The other lad had come to join us from his vigil because no one had come with the food and Aelfric had made his decision. He said he would return to the manor to see why we had been forgotten. We were to stay and watch the sheep and wait for his return. I was not at all happy with this and told him so. I wanted to go back with him. After a short but rather warm exchange of words I got my way. I was more surprised at this than I dared let on. Normally Aelfric was the one person who would not submit to my will, but that day he must have been more worried and distracted than I realized. This fact worried me more than anything else that had happened. If Aelfric was anxious then I had cause to be also.

We left the sheep folds almost immediately and quickly left them behind. The day was overcast and I remember thinking that the clouds looked ready to soak us both. In our haste to leave I had left my cloak at the hut and was not looking forward to a wet walk. Aelfric was very quiet and I reasoned that he was upset with my insisting that I should come along. I tried to talk to him, tried to apologize, but all I received in reply was a hollow grunt. His eyes never left the horizon. My gaze followed his and we both trudged onwards.

I remember looking ahead of us as we walked and thinking that we were in for a storm. The clouds were dark and leaden and ahead of us they seemed darker still. I could see a great patch of grey cloud directly in front of us.

We were only about two miles from the manor by this time and it was then that I noticed the shifting patterns in the clouds to our front. I stared, not wishing to believe what I was seeing. It was not cloud that darkened the sky ahead of us but smoke. It billowed up in great dark clouds to mix with the already grey sky. My mind began to race. Such a large amount of smoke could only mean one thing. A burning building. The manor? No, surely not. My mother was always so careful about such things. The church perhaps? The old priest was often clumsy and had set fire to things before now. Only the previous year he had fallen asleep without putting out his candle and it had only been a quick witted villager that had save both him and the church. Perhaps he had been unlucky this time. All these thoughts rushed through my mind as Aelfric and I quickened our pace and the black smoke rose ever upwards.

It can only have been a few minutes later, although it seemed like hours, when we crested the rise above the manor. The sight that met us was one that has haunted my dreams ever since and will stay with me until I am in my grave. The smoke, black now we were close to the source, covered half the sky and almost seemed to blot out the sun. It came from the village, a fact I had realized a little earlier as we approached the crest of the rise. I felt an immediate relief, thinking the manor was safe, and then a pang of guilt for my unthinking selfishness. I knew the villagers were even less capable of dealing with a fire than ourselves.

Nearly a mile away the village was in flames. Great black gouts of smoke snaked into the sky from the burning thatch and flames showed orange as they ate holes through the damp timbers. There did not seem to be one building that had escaped. As Aelfric and I stood watching the compelling spectacle my eyes were gradually dragged downwards. Downwards to the hollow in which the manor stood. Down to the blackened ruins of my home. Down to the bodies lying charred in the wreckage of the huts. Down to the gently smoking scene of carnage that was my family and servants. Down to the final death of my childhood.

I can remember but little of the next hours. We walked the last few hundred yards in a dazed silence. Aelfric, I think, was as stunned as I. We walked through the shattered remains of the gate, although the burnt stockade could have been crossed at any point, and gazed around in disbelief. Only single images remain of that dread sight. A jumble of pictures in my head, without sound or feeling. Just images. Agatha's Dane curled up by the gate, his hair singed and blood showing through his tunic. Agatha herself, a great blackened heap of burnt flesh in the embers of her shattered hut. No longer human but resembling more a roasted animal, her skin flayed in long crisp strips. A pot, shattered against the hearth, spilling out honey over the body of a dog. A table standing amidst the ruin still covered in a white cloth and set for a meal showing only dark marks from the fire. Ready for a meal that would never be eaten. One of the farm boys, his body limp as it hung on the broken spear shaft that pinned him to the remains of the well timbers. And my mother.

23

We found her outside the door of what remained of the hall. Her hair was unbraided and spilled loose about her face. She lay looking upwards on her back with her knees drawn back underneath her. She had been on her knees when the axe had hit her in the chest cleaving her like so much meat. Her eyes were wide and her teeth bared in terror. I could not look upon her face.

We did what we could for the dead, moving them all into what remained of the hall and covering them with whatever cloth we could find. Several bodies were unrecognisable and we could not move what remained of Agatha so left her where she lay. We worked all through the afternoon and into the evening finally lying down to sleep in the hall with the dead. They were our friends, we did not fear them.

I know now, as I lie here on my narrow cot awaiting the peace that sleep brings, that my life changed that night. To others it was just a small raid by a party of Danes eager to gain as much as they could before heading north but to me it was a gateway. A gateway into the world of men. I no longer was a child wishing for childish things but an individual person. I now harboured adult wishes, adult feelings. I wanted revenge and that need set the course for the rest of my life. I was so filled with hate that it would take thirty years of slaying to even slightly slake my thirst.
Perhaps somewhere an old Dane now sits and mourns for the death of his loved ones, a death at my hands - for God knows I slaughtered enough women and children in my time - and wonders at the reasons for our hatred, our savagery. Let him look back at my memories of that burnt out manor and tell me I had not the right. Let him answer for his murder and I will stand proud and answer for the deaths I returned upon them.

I was no saint and I own it readily enough, but then again I knew the man whose bones they now revere so highly and he was no more a saint than I. He saw the slaughter and felt as I did. He felt my grief and was touched by my anger. If saint he was, and who am I to deny all the priests of the land, then so were all who stood against the invaders. When he died it was not for some far flung ideal. It was not to protect the church, for they had as many Christians in their shield wall as heathens, but to stop such slaughter being meted out to other families such as mine. He died fighting the bastards that butchered my family and for me that is more than enough to ask of any man.

The fury of the Norsemen

'That year a great heathen force came into English land, and they took winter quarters in East Anglia; there they were horsed, and they [the East Anglians] made peace with them'.

So reads the Anglo-Saxon chronicle for the year 866 [2]. This 'Great heathen force' was to remain in England not just over the winter, as had previously been the case in the majority of such Danish raids, but permanently. Within five years it had defeated or intimidated into submission every army in England and caused the downfall of all the English kingdoms save Wessex. The Danes took York and destroyed the entire Northumbrian army, forced the Mercians to sue for peace and routed the forces of East Anglia killing Edmund, King of East Anglia, in the process.

Never before had a single army had such a catastrophic effect upon the Anglo-Saxon people of England. After centuries of domination it was the turn of the Anglo-Saxons to feel the threat of raiders from the sea. This 'Great heathen force' destroyed the old kingdom of East Anglia, united the Anglo-Saxons and created a saint who was to become one of the patrons of England and would be remembered long after the names of the victors had faded from memory.

And yet little is known of this campaign that resulted in the destruction of East Anglia and death of its king. Who were these invaders? How large was this 'Great Force'? Why did an entire kingdom's army fall to them and what were the causes?

The reasons for the Danish [3] invasion of England are multiple and complex. Their own homelands were becoming crowded and in countries such as Norway, where only the coastal strip could be farmed, this problem was even more acute. If the older children inherited the father's land the younger sons would have to find themselves land elsewhere to farm. For many the option of becoming a farmer was never available. They had to make their living from trading and travelling. Ibn Rustab, an Arab geographer, writing in approximately 920 A.D., gives us a vivid picture of the Norse traders he encountered during his travels.

'They have no villages, estates or fields. Their only occupation is trading in sable and squirrel and other kinds of skins, which they sell to those who will buy from them. They take coins in payment and fasten them to their belts. They are clean in their clothing and the men adorn themselves with gold arm rings'.

Ibn Rustab is one of the few writers to leave us a first hand account of the Viking peoples that is not coloured by fear or religious fervour. He may have found them a brutal people whom he found difficult to understand yet in all his writings his admiration for them as a race stands out. He states:-

'I have never seen more perfect specimens, tall as date palms, blond and ruddy. Each man has an axe, sword and a knife which he keeps with him at all times'.

It is almost difficult to accept that these "perfect specimens" so admired by Rustab were also the people who ransacked villages, sold their captives into slavery and butchered any who tried to stand against them. It is only when we start to look at other aspects of the Viking's world, and in particular their religion, that we can perhaps glimpse the root of their destructive natures.

The Viking's religion dictated a bloody way of life and the rise of a warrior cult meant that to die in battle was the greatest honour a man could attain. The philosophy of the Viking warrior is summed up in the poem 'Havemal' written in the ninth century:-

'Wealth dies,
Kinsmen die,
a man dies likewise himself;
but fame
never dies,
for him who gets good fame.
Wealth dies,
Kinsmen die,
a man dies likewise himself;
I know one thing
that never dies
the verdict on each man dead'.

This warrior cult was supported and encouraged by the religion prevalent throughout Scandinavia. A religion that worshiped warfare, death and the destructive forces of nature.The religion of the Vikings is colourfully brought to life by Adam of Bremen in his writings about the Temple of Uppsala in the mid eleventh century. He states that:-

'In this temple, entirely decked out in gold, the people worship the statues of three gods in such a way that the mightiest of them, Thor, sits on a throne in the middle of the chamber. Woden and Frey have places on either side. Thor rules over the wind, which controls the thunder and lightning, the winds and rain, fair weather and crops. The other, Woden carries on war and gives to man strength against his enemies. The third is Frey who gives peace and pleasure to men'.

Another factor which served to force the Danes from their homeland was the new found political stability in southern Scandinavia. From about the middle of the ninth century southern Norway, southern Sweden and Denmark were united under King Horik and this in turn restricted the action of some of the more adventurous local chieftains. Their response was to look across the oceans for new opportunities, adventure and profits. It began with raids on the northern isles and Ireland, returning home each winter, and ended with the attempted colonisation of all Britain.

The first recorded raid on the Anglo-Saxons was in 787 when a force of Northmen harried the coast of Dorset [4]. This was rapidly followed in 793 when the monasteries at Lindisfarne and Jarrow were brutally sacked. Described by Alcuin of York [5] as **'brutal robbery and slaughter'** this first attack was merely a foretaste of the destruction to come.

Although peace returned quickly after the attack on Lindisfarne the raids resumed in 835. These later attacks took the form of hit and run raids rarely pushing more than 15 miles inland giving the inhabitants little time to organise a defence before the raiders disappeared once more into the sea mists. These raids are described with vivid clarity by a Frankish author, Ermentarius of Noirmout, writing in the ninth century. He states that:-

'The number of ships increases, the endless flood of Vikings never ceases to grow. Everywhere Christ's people are victims of massacre, burning and plunder.... The Vikings over run all that lies before them and none can withstand them....Thus little by little is coming to pass the prophesy spoken by the lord through the mouth of his prophet [Jeremiah]; ' out of the north a scourge shall break forth upon all the inhabitants of the earth'.

In 851 the raids took on a new pattern.

Until this point the raiders had landed in the spring or early summer, looted the immediate area and returned home long before the onset of the winter. In 851 everything changed. The **'greatest force yet seen'** [6] landed in the kingdom of Kent, defeated the Mercian King who ruled there, destroyed Canterbury and then instead of boarding their ships for home set up camp and settled down for the winter.

The raid on Kent set a precedent for subsequent attacks. These raids from the sea were no longer small ship loads of fortune hunters on a summer campaign, but a large well equipped invasion force prepared to consolidate, if only temporarily, any area they captured. The Anglo-Saxon kings were no longer facing the annoying small incursions of fifteen years previously but facing a battle for their very survival.

Anglo-Saxon England

England at the time of the Danish invasion was a very different place from that which we know today. Made up of a group of independent kingdoms, the Anglo-Saxons ruled from north of Edinburgh to the south coast and as far west as Offa's Dyke. To the north lay the kingdom of Northumbria centered on York and stretching from the Firth of Forth to the Humber. Northumbria was at this time regarded as one of the centres of an Anglo-Saxon renaissance. It was here that Christianity first became widespread in Britain and here also that led a revival in architecture, craftsmanship and spiritual enlightenment not seen in Britain since the decline of Rome.

South of Northumbria the middle kingdom of Mercia held sway over several smaller kingdoms and was so wealthy that Charlemagne, the Frankish Emperor, treated its king as an equal. Lining the south coast was a series of kingdoms including Kent, Sussex and Wessex. Of these kingdoms Wessex was the most powerful and held the others under its control along with the ancient kingdom of Essex.

The oldest of the Anglo-Saxon kingdoms was East Anglia stretching from the river Stour, on the Essex/Suffolk border, north to the coast and west across most of the fens. The origins of the Kingdom are obscure but in the early seventh century, under King Redwald, whom Bede hailed as 'Bretwalda' or 'King of Britain' East Anglia dominated the other minor Anglo-Saxon kingdoms. It has been suggested that the ship burial at Sutton Hoo, which yielded so many awe inspiring treasures, was that of Redwald and if this is the case then it would indicate that East Anglia was truly a rich kingdom.

This appears to have been the peak of the kingdom's power and by the time of the Danish invasion East Anglia was a minor kingdom that had in turn been dominated by both Mercia and Wessex.

Although the kingdom of East Anglia was not the equal of Wessex or Mercia it was by no means unimportant. Dominance of the east coast and access to the continent made it a rich and cosmopolitan area. From ports such as Dunwich the products of the Saxons were transported to the Frankish kingdoms and goods from as far as the Middle East found their way into Saxon noble households. As a centre for trade and travel it was important to both Mercia and Northumbria and its fertile land made it an attractive target for any King wishing to expand his sphere of influence.

The population of the kingdom of East Anglia during the ninth century is difficult to estimate. Contemporary sources claim that much of the coastal area had become depopulated owing to the incursions of frequent Danish raids. The inhabitants had moved inland to seek safer settlements. The coast was no longer the province of the monks and holy men who had made their quiet retreats on its shore, but had become instead a place of terror.

Such was the fear inspired by these raids that in the small parish churches the peasants prayed **'From the fury of the Norsemen, good Lord, deliver us'**. This fear was not a shadowy fear of the unknown but a real fear of the violence and destructive force of the pagan Danes. It is recorded that during the sack of Peterborough one Dane slew eighty-four monks while another cut away the ribs of an English lord and pulled his lungs out while throwing salt into the wound. These invaders were a very real threat to the peoples of England.

The majority of these people were farmers and their families who made a reasonable living from the land. They settled in small villages that afforded them not just protection but also access to such people as traders, craftsmen and priests. Their houses were well built of wood and thatch furnished with tables and benches often of a high standard. Family life revolved around a central hearth that not only provided warmth but was also the main cooking area. Often several generations would live in the same building and although this might have been uncomfortable in larger families aged relatives were treated with great respect and reverance. The households were largely run by the women who were by no means limited to purely domestic matters. Women not only saw to the day to day running of a household but also appear to have played a large part in financial and business matters [7].

Many of the artefacts discovered from the period testify to a population with an eye for ornamentation and the resources to pay for quality. These were not a people scratching a living from the soil but a complex society with a relatively wealthy agricultural community as its very backbone. The free landholders paid taxes and in return could expect the protection of the law and the support of both church and king.

Although slaves were not unknown the great majority of the people were freeborn and had recourse to a system of justice not equalled again until the later middle ages. The law protected all men's property and persons by implementing a system of fines upon the guilty party. These fines were set upon a sliding scale and varied depending upon the type of crime and against whom it was commited. Each defendant would be called before an assembled court and witnesses for both sides would be heard before any judgement would be passed. So strict was the rule of law that testimony that was not supported by a witness would not be admissable in court [8].

If parties were not satisfied by the result of any case then, with the support of their kinsmen, they could appeal to the king himself. Such a system of course meant that the family of the injured party must not only stand by him but also have confidence in the right of his case. If they were proved wrong then they would also suffer the burden of compensation.

The result of this system seems to have been a society where family ties, hard work and the rule of law were respected by all classes. The East Anglia that Edmund ruled must have been a prosperous kingdom despite the ever present threat of the Danes.

The Witness.

I remember the events of the next morning with some clarity. I awoke to the strange sensation of one side of my body being cold and the other warm, a sensation now only too common to me but at the time unusual. I was lying next to Aelfric and we were both sharing what few covers were available. The night had been cold and my arm and leg that were furthest from the musky warmth of Aelfric's body were chilled to the bone.

I lay for several moments, my eyes closed, trying to remember all that had happened the previous day. I almost imagined that we were back in the sheep hut and it was only the stench of burnt wood and flesh that brought me back to the reality of the day and made me drag open my eyes.

I leapt to my feet and a startled cry escaped my lips. There were armed men in the remains of the yard. They seemed in those first moments, illuminated only by the grey predawn light, as dark ghosts of the warriors who had caused the destruction around me. Aelfric leapt to my side and laid a protective hand on my shoulder trying to put himself between the warriors and my shaking body. Then for what seemed an eternity nothing happened.

The warriors appeared as startled as we were. A strange sight we must have made, two figures rising from a line of corpses. I had seen one step backwards and hastily cross himself and the others just stared, making no move to advance. Then a voice called out from the other side of the yard. It was calling my name. Confusion claimed my mind and I did not understand what was happening. Who were these men? Why were they here? It was then that I recognised the one figure that moved towards us. Only a dark shape in the greyness but a shape that was familiar to me. As he drew close I struggled past the still motionless figure of Aelfric and ran into the outstretched arms of my father.

The next thing I can remember is sitting at a fire some distance from the wreckage of the manor. A cup was placed in my hands and a bittersweet liquid was poured into it. I drank without thought. My whole body and mind seemed numb and all around me seemed to be unreal. It all held a dreamlike quality and I watched all that went on with a mild detached interest.

My father was at my side at times, that I do remember. He covered my shoulders with a horse blanket and kept murmuring things into my unhearing ear. I mumbled some vague replies, I do not remember what, but he seemed satisfied. Aelfric sat opposite me. He had a different reaction to everything than I. He was weeping.

I had never seen Aelfric cry before, in fact I had never really seen him show any emotion other than the occasional grin or short gruff laugh. Now he wept as if there was no end to it. My father tried to console him but all seemed to no avail. He would not be comforted. Occasionally he would raise his face to my father's and, still weeping, cry that it was all his fault, that he should never have left them. My father could only place an arm around the old man's shoulders and gently stroking his matted hair trying to soothe him like a babe. It was the first time I realised that Aelfric was an old man.

I must have slept then, for the weak sun was high in the sky when next I awoke. I still felt groggy but my earlier stupor seemed to have worn off a little. Aelfric slept, curled into a tight ball and covered by a blanket, on the far side of the now dying fire.

The soldiers had been busy while I slept away the day. The bodies had been moved from the remains of our hall and now lay, decently shrouded, in a great long line awaiting burial. Beyond the shattered remains of the manor I could see a group of warriors, stripped to the waist in the chill air, attacking the ground with mattocks and spades. A grave pit was being dug.

As I stumbled my way towards the group, my eyes still bleary with sleep, my father noticed my approach and came forward to meet me. His face was drawn and great dark rings showed beneath his eyes. He and his men had ridden through the night following the wake of the destruction caused by a few rogue raiders from the Danish army. The King was moving further to the north with a larger force to put an end to the menace from the sea. The main army, still camped to the south, hemmed the raiders in to their river inlets and blocked their passage inland. The situation was under some control, or so my father said, but a look of deadened menace lay behind his eyes and it was obvious to me that he thought things were far from well.

Later, when we had time to talk, he explained that we were in a worse situation than the King wanted his followers to know. We were heavily outnumbered and the raiders were being reinforced almost daily as more ships joined their party. The King could only hope to buy a peace for the summer and hope that either the army would move on the following year or that Wessex or Mercia would come to our aid. If we had to keep the army in readiness all year then the harvest, which already looked far from good, would be a disaster and the money used to buy off the Danes would look meagre when compared to such a loss as that would incur. The king was trying desperately to look stronger than he really felt for the sake of his people and to deceive the enemy.

I felt at the time that my father was taking the loss of his wife and household very well. He seemed more concerned with the military situation than with his personal tragedy and this I found hard to understand. Looking back now I can see that this was just his way of dealing with his sorrow. If he threw all of his energies into this one thing then he would have no time to grieve. I think he also felt that he had no right to spend time in sorrow when his was merely one of several manors burnt on the northern coast. His job was to defend the shore and make sure that no other settlements suffered the same fate. I can understand this now, but at the time I felt that his detachment was a sign of disinterest. As events were to show I could not have been more mistaken.

The afternoon was spent burying the dead. They were placed in the shallow scrape made by the warriors and earth was piled over the bodies. My father ordered that large stones be carried up from the shore and placed on top to make it more difficult for scavengers to get at the corpses. Two of the bodies we did not bury. I had not noticed before but two of the bodies were that of raiders killed in the attack on the manor. These my father had staked out on the rise above the village and sent one of his axemen to remove their heads. These grisly trophies were thrown into the sea so that their souls would wander the earth forever in torment.

When all these gruesome tasks were complete the warriors settled down to prepare a meal. They seemed to be in little hurry to move on and when I enquired of my father the reason for this relaxed attitude he told me that we were waiting for the King.

Even in my disturbed state this caused some excitement in me. I had never before met my namesake. Oh, I had seen him from a distance, most people who had spent time in Thetford would have seen him in passing at one time or other, but I had never actually met the man my father so admired. The king had been with my father when he had arrived at the burnt out manor and had moved on with his men before it was realized that not all the bodies in the hall were as dead as they seemed. He had already commiserated with my father over my death. I felt a little aggrieved at this. Being cast over so easily.

The King arrived, as he had promised, with the setting of the sun. I was busy trying to get Aelfric to eat something at the time, to no avail, and the band of horsemen were already halfway down the slope before I noticed their approach. They came from the west and the setting sun was behind them, making it difficult to make out any details. What I could see was impressive. The King obviously meant to put a stop to the coastal raids for he had a force of some three hundred mounted warriors with him. News of their presence should at least deter any similar attacks and the sight of them would give heart to all who lived on the shore. The horses were guided down the slope at a gentle trot, a soft jangling coming from their harness, and circled round to the point where my father had tethered his mounts.

I left Aelfric to his meal. He showed no interest in the riders or me for that matter, so I left him and went to join my father in greeting his master.

As I approached the newly arrived troops I began to feel disheartened. I could not make out the King amongst them and feared he had returned to the army in the south. My father was in conversation with several of the riders but neither of the two main men matched the image I had in my mind of the noble figure from Thetford. The King was a soft faced man, his skin pale and his curled hair long and silken, or so my memory said. These men were both haggard, filthy-looking creatures, caked in mud, and with wild unkempt hair. Their gear was well made but all had a shabby, soiled look to it. I am sure my disappointment showed as I trudged over to stand at my father's side.

All conversation stopped at my arrival and my father and the two strangers turned to look at me. Unsure what was expected of me I gave a weak grin and looked at my father for his lead. He returned my stare with a look of puzzlement. "Is that any way to greet your King?" he said.

I am sure that my mouth was hanging loose as I returned my eyes to the other two figures. Both were laughing at my confusion and even my father managed a smile. The younger of the two stooped down onto one knee and clasped me by the shoulders. His face I could now see was soiled with grime and he smelt of horses and leather, but beneath the drab exterior I could just recognise the elegant man from Thetford. His face broke into a broad grin and he said " I hope I do not disappoint you child. I would hate it if my namesake felt I was not enough of a king for him".

The actual words, now I look back on them, meant very little, but the effect they had on me was profound. He had said them just to put me at my ease, realizing all I had been through he wished for no extra torment to befall me. From that moment onwards I was his man.

He had a knack at such things, my King Edmund, and he knew exactly when to use it. Certainly he could be stern and aloof, every inch a king in his bearing, but he knew when a kind word would get results quicker and with more ease. He was not as calculating as I make him sound. He was just a kind man who wished for his people to like as well as respect him. If he had a fault then it was only that he was at times too kind.

That day, standing amongst the ruins of my shattered home, he got it exactly right. No matter what came afterwards it is that first meeting that I will always remember and with the memory comes the feeling of warmth for the man. He could have turned his back there and then, never spoken another word to me, and still I would have been devoted to him.

We camped that night around the broken stockade and left as the sun rose the next morning.

The next week went by in a blur. I was taken by my father to join the main army in the south. We arrived in the evening and, after finding me a rough shelter to sleep in, my father left me to my own devices while he joined the king in council. I was begining to feel the hurt and loss of all that had happened in the previous few days and could not rest for much of the night. The surroundings did little to help my feelings of disorientation. It was the first time I had been in a soldiers camp and, to my untrained eyes, all seemed to be chaos and confusion. Fires burnt in all directions, as far as I could see through the smoke, and the ground was littered with hastily erected huts and tents. The camp was never quiet and even at midnight the sound of horses or the restless soldiers drifted through the night air. How anyone could make sense of the chaos was beyond me - a small, smelly haphazard city dumped onto the uplands above the marshes.

I spent several days in the camp before my father sent me to Thetford and the relative safety of our hall in the city. Aelfric was sent along as well being too old to be of much use to the army. He had regained some of his old self during our stay with the army and although still quiet and withdrawn he seemed to be reconciled to the events of the previous week. I think it was as much being amongst soldiers again as my fathers insistence that no blame lay with him that finally brought him round. On our last morning in camp I had watched him

33

teaching several of the younger warriors the best way to turn a spear thrust without using a shield. They all stood around and readily took aboard the advice that his experience gave, much as I had sat and listened to his stories. On our trip to Thetford he carried a spear and on his back hung a newly acquired shield. Aelfric had decided that if ever he had the chance he would revenge himself upon the heathen.

Little chance either of us had of revenge for our trip was uneventful and we were soon among the caring and solicitous servants who formed my father's household in the city. They were as shocked by the happenings by the sea as we ourselves were. Nearly all had family who had died and they were anxious to know what had happened. Aelfric, reluctant to impart the tale, told them that he would tell the story only once so that evening the whole household gathered after supper and the story was told. Aelfric spun his usual magic and had it not been a story of such sorrow to all who listened they would have admired his skill as a teller of tales. He left out all that was a horror to listen to yet still managed to convey what had happened with a crystal clarity. When he finished we were a household in mourning.

The next months passed in a sombre silence. All within the household were submerged in their own grief and it was not a pleasant place to be. The summer advanced and grew hot and the city began to reek of the foul odours caused by communal life. The mud in the road dried into hard ridges before finally being broken down into a fine reddish dust that caked clothing and clung to the back of the throat. The smell from the shit pits and the tanneries grew stronger and the atmosphere was tense. Late in June a small fire destroyed several outbuildings belonging to a farm just outside the stockade and town ditch. The town was alive with rumours of Danish spies and this did little to relieve the tension.

Much of the army had been sent home early in the summer but the King had retained a hard core of his best troops to keep an eye on the heathens. A peace had been made and these troops were there to make sure it was kept. My father was among these and we saw little of him throughout June or July, and as the weather grew hotter we began to feel the lack of a strong hand to guide the household. All the servants were irritable and the slightest thing could set off a huge row. I was of little use in preventing these outbursts for it was, more often than not, Aelfric who started the argument. If I tried to intervene he would merely look offended. He believed that we were bound together and that I should always back him even when I knew him to be wrong. This was causing some tension between us and it was only the fact that Aelfric was called away by my father that stopped us having a serious falling out.

Aelfric had been recalled to the camp above the marsh because my father felt that his experience would be of some use in drilling the newly raised levy troops. Edmund was raising section after section of his general militia and attempting to give each unit some training before he must disband them to return to their crops. Each unit was given about a month's instruction but as professional warriors were in short supply ancients such as Aelfric had been drafted in to fill the gaps. I am sure that this must have been of little use to the levy, there is no substitute for real combat, but it did Aelfric a power of good. When he returned to us in Thetford, at the beggining of the Autumn, he was his old self again.

His return was an occasion of joy for me, I had grown bored of the city and the loss of my mother weighed heavily upon me, but for others it was tinged with sadness. We had heard that several skirmishes had taken place with men of the heathen army but had thought little of it. The peace, signed by Edmund in the spring, still officially held but encounters between the more adventurous warriors from either side was inevitable. During one of these little clashes two of my father's household had been hurt. One, the son of my father's steward had died almost immediately, but the other, a town dweller called Sigurd, was now brought back home by Aelfric. He had taken a rough gash in his leg from a Danish spear and, although he was hale enough, the wound would not knit together properly. As the harvest was about to begin and Aelfric's job for the moment complete, he had been detailed to bring Sigurd back where he could rest and recover fully in the warmth of our hall.

Sigurd was not the only extra baggage that Aelfric returned with. Along in his party came a pair of women. The younger, a girl of about thirteen called Elinor, was the child of my father's cousin who was now left orphaned after his death. My father had felt it his duty to take them in even though she had little money and even less land. My father's cousin was a wastrel who lost almost all he had paying fines to the king of Mercia for the death of three of his servants. No common servants, you understand, but men of the King's own household stupid enough to try and cheat on the throw board. Had he not died when he did, my father said, the Mercians would have taken the rest as well. Along with Elinor came a lot of extra baggage including her nurse, a spiteful old bitch called Ida.

Elinor was a sweet child, several years my senior, and already showing that, for her, womanhood lay a few short years ahead. This fact did not escape the notice of her nurse who fussed about her as though she was about to be raped by every man she saw. It was difficult to even exchange a polite word with the girl without getting a sharp crack round the head from the ever vigilant Ida. After my first attempts at polite friendship had been thus dealt with I retired from the fray and let them do much as they wished. Not so for old Aelfric.

For some reason I could not even hazard a guess at, Aelfric had taken a liking to the old nurse. To all others she appeared a spiteful old harridan best left well alone yet to Aelfric she was womanhood incarnate. In short, he loved her. I never saw her say a kind word to the man but the more she spurned him the more he adored her. I am sure now that she did hold some kindness in her stony heart for Aelfric but she was so used to expressing her love with stern words and harsh advice that she used the same method on him. He revelled in it.

This strange shift of events caused me some concern and I came to resent Ida with all my heart. Where death and fire had failed to take him away from me I now saw Ida putting an insurmountable barrier between us. How he could bear to be in her company when he could have been with me instead I found hardest to understand. I felt rejected and more alone than at any time since the raid on the manor. In turn I rejected Aelfric and Ida and, to some extent, Elinor.

It was difficult to wholly reject Elinor though for she now found herself in a similar position to myself. She had lost all that was familiar to her, been thrust into new and strange circumstances, and now faced losing the one stable individual in her life to an amorous old soldier. I could sympathize with her, but only from a distance. Ida saw to that.

And so we all spent a most unusual winter in Thetford. It was not a harsh year but it was a wet one. The roads never seemed to dry out completly and this made travel difficult and tiresome. We saw my father only half a dozen times that year and I suppose that since the day I had left the army's camp I had spent less than a month in his company. He did, however, manage to return to Thetford for the winter feast and to help me celebrate my eleventh birthday.

All I remember really is that it was warm and damp and that the mud managed to get everywhere. It seemed an impossible task even keeping my feet dry and I was permanently clammy. My father rode in the day before the feast and rode out the day afterwards. He had not been expected to return so the steward had not prepared anything special for the main meal, birthdays being little thought of, and my father was most annoyed. He had a worn, tired look about him and I felt that he was always restless. Just as he settled in one place he would be up and moving around again. Perhaps just a reaction to the constant need to be on his guard when with the army. It did not make for a very happy day.

I can still clearly remember certain things though, as all children do, and that was the gifts. I cannot of course recollect all that was given to me, for in a large household the lord's son was likely to recieve many gifts, but three things still remain clear. The first was a spear given me by the noble Aelfric. It was not of course full sized but it had a wickedly sharp blade as long as my forearm and he must have spent many hours polishing the ash shaft with beeswax for it shone like amber. The second was from Elinor. A belt that she had woven herself, and although not perfect it meant a lot to me for I knew how she hated weaving with the rough tablets. I wore it until it finally fell apart several years later and I think that pleased her greatly.

The third gift was brought to me by my father. It was not from him, I cannot truly remember what he gave me, but from the King himself. As I have said, Edmund was ever a kind man and he remembered that my birth coincided with the day of his crowning and the winter feast. He must have remembered me from our meeting in the spring and wished to show the small, sad child some kindness. I was more touched by the thought than by the actual gift, the fact he remembered me at all made me feel in some way special, and the small silver crucifix on its fine chain became, for me at least, a symbol of my devotion to him.

It is odd how such a small bauble can become an object of great value. True it had a value in itself, for it was finely made and was etched with a vine pattern, but to me its worth far outweighed its monetary value. I still wear it today, although the etching wore down many years ago, and it is probably my most highly prized possession.

With the coming of spring came the renewed threat from the invader's army. The peace still held but for how long no one knew, if it was to be broken then it would happen soon. Edmund sent a call out for a general muster and for several weeks Thetford became the centre of activity as the newly raised levy gathered itself before moving off to join the main army. It was a time of excitement for me and sleepless nights, I had never seen so many armed men and the streets were thronged with warriors. For others it was a time of worry. I learnt later that Edmund had sent messages to both the kings of Mercia and Wessex seeking their support for a campaign against the heathens but no help came. Mercia had problems of its own, their northern border was threatened by civil war in Northumbria, and they could not release troops to come to our aid. Wessex also refused help, they feared an attack on their own coasts and so were busy seeing to their own defences. If the Danes broke the peace then we would be on our own.

Early that year the invaders made their move. To our great relief and suprise it was not against us. They marched their army west, constantly shadowed by Edmund's forces, and crossed the fen causeway into Mercia. From there they travelled north and lay siege to York, the capital of Northumbria.

Nowadays all know what happened next but at the time it took us many months to find out. Rumours flew around only to be contradicted the very next day by an equally incorrect tale. Mercia had fallen. The Danes had been slaughtered to a man. The truth was much more interesting.

The Northumbrians had been busy killing each other when the army had arrived and it was only after York had fallen at the beginning of November that they realized the extent of the threat. Eventually joining forces they five months later attacked the heathens at York. They broke through the defences of the fort, but once inside found themselves outnumbered and were soon overcome. The slaughter was very great. We heard that most of the noble families in the kingdom had been all but wiped out and that it had taken the Danes a full week just to remove the bodies from the fort. The Danes also had suffered, that much we knew, but to what extent they were weakened we had no idea.

Both rival Northumbrian kings were killed in the struggle and it was left to the few surviving nobles to make a peace with the invaders. I found the whole event shocking. It shook my belief in all that I thought to be true. I knew of Northumbria as a great and powerful kingdom, a people whom even the powerful Mercians respected. If such a mighty kingdom could be all but destroyed in less than a year then what would become of the rest of us? Now the Danes had a kingdom at their command they could be reinforced from across the sea almost at will and we might have to face an even larger army. I almost expected the invaders to start sweeping south into Mercia immediately. When nothing happened and the invaders appeared to have settled down at York I began to feel a little less worried.

As I have said, none of this was really known to us at the time. We picked up pieces of news as they became available. Thetford was a great trade centre and most information was spread by the tradesmen and merchants who had the opportunity for travel. Those coming east from Mercia had the most reliable news but still we would hear other snippets of gossip from travellers from the south. My father, who had returned to Thetford shortly after Edmund had disbanded his army, took all these stories at face value and would believe whatever the latest rumour said until it was contradicted by a more recent story.

This inability by my father to see through even the most obvious falsehood often puzzled me. I suppose that it was one of the reasons why he was so respected in the courts of law. He could always see both sides of the argument and, to tell the truth, many of the rumours that were dismissed by all but my father turned out to hold the seed of truth within. Who but he could have believed, without reservation, that such a mighty kingdom as Northumbria could have been all but destroyed in just under a year. It was my father's ability to sift through a veritable mountain of conflicting rumours and find the consistent kernel of truth that led to my next prolonged encounter with King Edmund.

You must first understand the state that Edmund's kingdom was in before you can really appreciate the far-sightedness of his actions. East Anglia had been badly affected by the invader's year long stay within our borders. They had drained the royal treasury of what little reserves it ever held and had severely curtailed opportunity for trade. I know that our family lost much in the way of wealth to their war bands and I also know that we had come off lightly compared to some. We still had several untouched holdings and the sheep flocks had been left virtually intact. Others had not been so lucky. This had not just affected the wealth of the kingdom but had also affected the wellbeing of the people as a whole.

People were scared. They had good reason to be. With Northumbria gone they began to realise the threat that all the English kingdoms lay under. True Northumbria had been a divided, war torn kingdom at the time of defeat but were we in a much better position? The rumours coming from all directions sent some people into panic and had everybody on edge. Edmund knew that if he was to rebuild the strength and confidence of his people then he must know exactly what was going on. With this in mind he did two things. Firstly, he sent out a series of spies into Mercia and Northumbria. They would send back irregular messages of what was happening and hopefully give him some time to react to any future events. Secondly, he set up a system of border patrols. Members of his own bodyguard would control a series of outposts along the entire western border of the kingdom and keep a wary eye on traffic crossing our borders and an ear open for new rumours. If the first series of spies failed in their duty then at least the second line of border guards would give some warning.

This is of course how I see it today. I do not know Edmund's exact reasons for his actions but I think that I knew him well enough to guess at his motives. Whatever they were they meant a great change for me.

My father was put in command of a large section of the border, from the northern sea south to Ely, and this meant that once again he was to be away from the hall at Thetford. As he was to be away, and knew not for how long, he decided it best that I should not be left to my own devices with just Elinor for company. This was the summer before my twelfth birthday and as my education was somewhat lacking, my father blaming it on the war, it was decided that I should be placed in the royal household for as long as my father was away. For me this all came as a great suprise. I had been so long running almost wild in my father's hall that I thought that it would always be so. My education consisted of a few hours a week with the steward, spear practice with the other lads of the area and long talks with Aelfric. I considered this to be as much as any young man needed and would have happily forgone the time spent with the steward. To be sent away into another household, even though it was a bare two miles away, and be educated by the priests seemed a heavy punishment. So it was with a mixture of fear and resentment that at the end of July I was taken by my father to the King's hall.

To tell the truth living in the King's household soon became more of a pleasure to me than a bane. It was an easy life that was little different from my time spent in my father's hall. True, there was a little more time spent in the company of the priests than I felt the need for but otherwise it was most enjoyable. Being a member of the royal household, even such an insignificant member, gave me a much more inflated opinion of myself. I see now that when I returned home, as I did occasionally when my father returned from the border, I must have seemed an arrogant young brat. All was always bigger and better within the King's household, or so I said, and I felt that my visits to home somehow demeaned me. I began to notice that rather than me avoiding Elinor and Ida it was them avoiding me. In my new found arrogance I surmised that they were merely jealous of my new found status. I suspect now that I just bored them.

For me though, everything was bigger and better in Edmund's household. When not actually being taught by the priests the other boys and I could do much as we wanted. No one took much notice of the boys running around and it was only when I got in someones way or did something particularly vile that I was even visible to the eyes of the ever busy court. And it was a very busy time indeed. Edmund's system of spies was beginning to work and there were always fresh riders entering the stableyards with news for the King and his council. News would come in, scribes would be summoned, meetings held and fresh orders go out. All was action and the feeling around the whole hall was always one of controlled energy. The other boys and I of course knew very little of what was actually going on. We heard all the usual rumours and exchanged gossip with any of the servants that were willing to talk to us but we found out very little of interest.

The major advantage to living in the King's hall, or so I thought at the time, was that I would see more of the King himself. In practice this was not really true. Edmund was a young, vigorous monarch who had a great deal to do in a very short space of time. He was more often than not away from court, patrolling his outposts, seeing his people and in turn being seen. He was never away for more than a week or so but when he returned he would be closeted with his scribes and councillors for days at a time before riding out once more. I am sure that it was only Edmund's personal energy and enthusiasm that kept up the momentum of preparation and training throughout that dark period. And dark it was for we expected the next Danish attack to fall on our borders. We were the weakest kingdom in England and expected no mercy to be shown to us. So it was a great suprise to us all when we heard that the Danish army, reinforced and re-equiped, had launched an invasion of Mercia.

I say it was a suprise to us and by that I mean to the general populace, Edmund most likely had news of their intentions almost as soon as the Mercians themselves. His network of spies was well established by this time.

I remember the day when it all began to happen, when we began to fight back. I had been at spear practice with several of the other lads in the stockyard behind the hall. We had to drill here for the steward would not let us use the main courtyard. He claimed that we were so poor in our practice that we distracted the other servants and set them to laughing. This was most unfair for if their was one thing we did enjoy working at it was practice at arms. For my age and size, I was still a little scrawny, I was considered to be a most promising warrior and all of us resented the steward's mocking.

That day we had finished our lessons with the monks somewhat earlier than was usual, there were many more reports to write, and we were released to our instruction about noon. We had spent longer than usual practicing and as the afternoon drew to a close we all lounged, red faced and sweaty, against the stockade wall. It was early in the spring after my twelfth birthday and the weather was mild and damp. The stockyard was ankle deep in mud and now it was gradually drying into a solid mass around my feet. As we sat, trying to look manly and fierce, the gates were suddenly flung open. At the entrance rode in a party that was so bedraggled it made our muddy little group look positively clean. It was Edmund returned from his latest inspections.

The group was somewhat larger than normal. Edmund had obviously picked up some of his messengers as he returned home. Most of these men I at least recognised for it was considered by the children a great honour to be in their company and we dogged their heels whenever they returned. But this time they had some strangers amongst them. Several of the strange horsemen were obviously of high rank and the one that seemed to lead them wore the boar-crested helmet of a Mercian. Quickly we were shouted across to help the grooms, the arrival of the large party had obviously caught them unawares, and we all jumped to help.

The other lads threw down their spears and trotted and splashed their way across to the horses but I was unwilling to leave my spear behind. It was the one Aelfric had made for me and I knew that several of the other lads had their eyes upon it. So I followed on behind still carrying my spear. By the time I arrived most of the horses had been taken hold of and I, for some reason, was left to hold the leading Mercian's beast. I had been heading for Edmund's horse but had been pushed out of the way by the head groom so I had grabbed the nearest bridle. Edmund and the Mercian were still in the saddle, the Mercian was talking to the King and I found his rough accent harsh and even a little difficult to understand. Edmund sat impassively, he looked more tired than I had ever seen him before, but his eyes showed that he was listening and taking in all that was going on around him. The conversation over, the stranger moved to dismount but then let forth a peal of laughter. Edmund also halted, obviously

40

wondering what the Mercian found so amusing, and I discovered that it was towards me that the laughter was directed.

All eyes were on me. I could feel the colour begin to rise in my face yet had no idea what it was that caused his laughter. The Mercian turned back to the king and said "I see that you really are more prepared for a fight than even I expected. Now you have armed even the stableboys".

Those were, as well as memory serves, the exact words he spoke to the King that afternoon. If he had said them to any other, or if I had left my spear behind with the rest, then my life would have been very different. Often I have wondered how so much can be changed by such a simple statement and sometimes when I am in the depths of blackness I wish they had never been said. But said they were and it was a changing point in my whole life. Of course, I did not know that at the time, I just felt embarassed and a little hurt. Firstly to be mistaken for a stable boy and then to have myself and my lovely spear laughed at was almost too much to bear. It was Edmund who came to my defence.

In a glance Edmund took in my situation and his tired face broke into a half smile. He could sense my discomfiture and knew that the story of the armed stableboy would have circulated the entire court by dark and he understood the hurt that it would cause me. His reply was clipped, swift and sure.

Looking down upon me he said "That is no stableboy but rather Edmund, son of one of my hearthguard, and one of my armour bearers. It is to him that Mercia will have to ask support from in the future. He will be a strong warrior and so, if you do not wish to spend your old age as a hunted fugitive I would ask his forgiveness from him now, while he is still young enough to take a joke rather than a life."

This seemed to amuse all the horsemen and laughter echoed around the wooden palisade. I hardly remember what the Mercian replied. That he apologised I have no doubt but my mind was still reeling from what Edmund had just said. I was to be an armour bearer. Several of the other lads looked on open mouthed. I could hardly take it in. Me, a mere twelve years old, to become an armour bearer.

To understand my reaction you must understand what an armour bearer was. Since the Danes came to this land it has ceased to be the position of honour that it once was and is now a duty carried out by servants. The duty itself was simple. It was to care for and carry the personal arms of your lord, but the honour it bestowed was great. It was a post normally reserved for the sons of high ranking nobles who were approaching the age when they would take their place in the shield wall. For me to be shown such a distinction at such an early age was almost unheard of. I have often wondered if Edmund regretted his hasty words but the word of the King is final and to retract his offer would have been great shame for both me and my father. Hasty words spoken to save a young lads pride but once said there was no going back. I was to be an armour bearer to King Edmund.

At first I did think that Edmund had forgotten what he had promised me in the stableyard for no one came to show me my new duties and when I enquired of the steward what I should do he churlishly told me exactly what I could do. Everything about the King's hall was in disorder at that time. My aimless wandering in search of my new duties did enable me to find out exactly what was going on but I did not really understand the importance of the events.

The Mercians had sent their envoys to Edmund in search of help. They were under attack and the Danes had laid a siege at Nottingham that the Mercians did not feel confident enough to try and break without help. They had sent to all of their neighbouring kingdoms in search of extra troops and royal support and the envoy that now sat with Edmund in the great hall was merely one of many that we received over the next few months.

Edmund was unwilling to commit his troops to the fight without first knowing the intentions of Wessex. If he joined with Mercia without Wessex also joining he risked a defeat from the newly reinforced Danish army and that would leave his own kingdom defenceless. Edmund needed reassurance.

This may sound a harsh and cold hearted decision now but at the time it made a lot of sense. Why risk a fight before we were fully ready? Anyway, we could remember little support coming from Mercia when we had needed it the previous year. Let the Mercians buy a peace with the enemy and give us all time to prepare. This time it would be Mercian gold and not East Anglian that the Danes would be taking home. Some of the older warriors still considered Mercia to be the enemy and I know that they secretly laughed at the Mercian's plight.

As it was, God willed things differently. Over the next few weeks all about the court was activity and news. Mercian envoys would arrive hot on the heels of Edmund's own spies, messengers from Wessex and Kent would halt only long enough to pass letters to the king. All was excitement and bustle. We heard first that Nottingham had fallen and was being newly defended by the Danes then, only a few days later, we heard that Wessex was sending troops to help the beleagured Mercians.

This last piece of news was what finally decided Edmund upon a course of action. The very night that the messenger arrived Edmund sent out his own scouts. The army was to be called up and mustered within the week.

This was an impossibly short space of time to gather the entire army and Edmund knew it. The supplies alone would take longer than that to be brought together. Edmund was only expecting to have the main group of his professional warriors ready and with them he could at least show willing and give some support to the other armies. He was gambling. He was gambling that if the army of Wessex was already on the way, and our reports stated that it was, then the Danes would have word of it. If they then heard that Edmund was gathering his forces as well they might think better of facing all three kingdoms at once, even from behind secure defences.

As is now well known the gamble paid off. Edmund's main army was still only half formed, and he and his advance troops only just over the border into

Mercia, when the news arrived that the Danes had signed a peace and were preparing to return north once more. The army was once more sent home without spilling a single drop of blood.

Edmund did not return immediately but carried on to Nottingham to meet with the leaders of the other armies. Burgred, king of Mercia was there and Alfred, brother of the king of Wessex, was also present. What went on at that meeting I never found out but when Edmund returned several weeks later he seemed more relaxed and in better spirits than I had seen him in for many months.

With the disbanding of the army and Edmund's return things began to slowly return to normal. The priests spent less time closeted with the king and so I and the other lads had to return once more to our lessons. After all the excitement of the summer this was most difficult and I am sure that we were less than ideal students for the long suffering tutors. We were forever attempting to escape their charge and would disappear at the slightest excuse. We taunted each other, answered back and generally showed them as little respect as we could get away with. The warmth of the autumn weather made us even more irritable and on several occasions only stern warnings from the strong armed steward kept us in any semblance of order. And so it was that at the end of a particularly irksome day that I found myself summoned before the steward.

I was sure that I was in for a thrashing. I could not work out why I had been singled out for such discipline but had no doubt that I deserved it. I had been foul to all three of our tutors within the space of as many days and added to that I had been caught taking apples that were being stored in one of the hay lofts. At the time the servant who had cornered me in the barn, still clutching my ill-gotten prizes, had merely cuffed me round the head and sent me packing but I now reasoned he had informed on me to the steward and I was determined to repay the compliment at the earliest opportunity.

To my suprise when I was finally let into the steward's dark, timber scented hut he seemed to be in a rather good mood. He sat on a bench against one wall with his feet on a stool and told me to come and sit beside him. I quickly obeyed. Now I was really worried. This kind treatment was usually reserved for the smaller boys when they were about to be told that they had suddenly become orphans. Had something happened to my father I asked. He replied that nothing had happened and that all was well. It was simply that he had been informed by the king that I was to be trained as an armour bearer and would, from that point onwards, live with the two other older boys who already fulfilled the task and finally earn my keep. I was still to attend lessons with the priests but I must now consider myself a working member of the household and would be his responsibility. When he had finished his little prepared speech I simply sat dumbly next to him staring at the further wall. Edmund had not forgotten his promise made in the spring.

And so began the worst time that I ever spent in Edmund's household. My few personal possesions were moved into the small, rather smelly hut that I was to share with the other two lads and I was set to work. This I did not mind at all, the work was easy and took little time each day and I think that I even paid more attention to the priests' monotonous dronings. The trouble was with the

43

other two lads. These days I cannot even remember their names but both were several years my senior and hated everthing about me. They resented sharing their already cramped conditions and further resented the fact that I had been singled out to join them by the king himself. They saw me as an undersized brat who, by just being there, would undermine their position of honour in the household. They did not mind the work I did, that you can be sure of, and very soon I found myself doing most of their share as well as my own.

Things were made much worse by the fact that Edmund often singled me out for praise. As armour bearers we had to attend upon him several times a week and often as not he would spare the time to exchange a few words with me. I suspect that he always had a soft spot for the weaklings and his kindness, although a balm to my wounds at the time, would be paid for later on in the privacy of the hut. After three months of this hell on earth I had come close to my limits and considered running back to my father's hall in the city. I am sure it was only the obvious hurt and shame that this would have caused my family that stopped me. Nevertheless my thirteenth birthday was passed in a state of ill humour and I could see little to improve my lot in the near future.

But just when I had reached what I thought to be my lowest point things started to get better. My own little miracle happened. Firstly the spring arrived. No miracle I grant you, but the arrival of the spring always did, and still does, lift my heart. I could spend less time within doors and in the company of the other two lads and get outside into the fresh clean air. Secondly, I began to grow. I had always been small for my age, and this had been a disadvantage that the other two had played upon, but all of a sudden I began to shoot up like a young sapling. I grew at an almost alarming rate and my tunics were almost too small for me by the time they were finished. My fellow armour bearers suddenly became a little wary of giving me the slaps and kicks that I had become so used to.

The third little miracle was by far and away the best. Elinor returned to my life. To be truthful she had never really left it, for I saw her whenever I made the short trip to my father's hall, but now she came to join me in the royal household. She was almost sixteen years old now and had fullfilled all her early promise by developing into a real beauty. She had been sent to serve in the queen's household and as she knew very few people at the court she sought me out upon every occasion. The effect this had on the other two lads was even more startling than my rapid growth. They were both, very obviously, smitten with her and would do all in their power to please her even if this meant being pleasant to me.

To tell the truth I too was smitten by Elinor. I believe most of the young men at court were. She was truly a wonder to behold. She was one of those dark girls whose beauty lay in her long dark hair and eyes that a man could drown in. Her features taken individually were not particularly fine but when seen as a whole they made me believe that there was not a finer looking girl in all of the eastlands. Her body too was something to marvel at for, although still only sixteen, she was developing a fine figure. This I discovered one afternoon as I was cleaning out the hut I shared with the other two lads.

44

It was a warm day and I had been volunteered to miss my afternoon at weapons practice to air all the bedding and generally tidy the mess that three young men can create. I had removed most of the items outside and now squatted against one of the inner walls wasting away the afternoon. Elinor came through the open door at a rush and almost tripped over my feet for in spite of her looks and bearing she was still inclined to being clumsy. This was obviously not the first accident she had had that afternoon for her gown was covered with what can best be described as a filthy mess. She explained that she had been sent from the kitchen, a lean-to butted against the wall of the main hall, to take a dish of curds to the steward. She did not know how it had come to pass but she had managed to drop the whole dishful down her front and needed to change into her best dress. At that time Elinor was having similar troubles to my own with the other girls in the household and, girls being what they are, she now stored some of her more prized possessions in my little hut. She quickly stripped off her belt and dress and rummaged around in my newly created mess looking for her bundle. What she did not realise was that she was standing with the light behind her and even though she still wore her shift I could see more than she would have liked.

My memory is vague upon the subject these days but I do remember being most disturbed with the view and I could not keep my mind to my task for the rest of the afternoon. I looked at her in a different light from that day forward and probably became more of a hindrance to her than both the other lads put together. I suppose it was love. Not the gradually acquired gentle love that I later shared with my wife but the all consuming, mind numbing love that is first love. Whatever you may call it and however I may describe it, I know that it seriously affected my view of the next year. All was suddenly right with the world, my surroundings heavenly and even my companions tolerable. I went through my training in a daze and my eyes would ever be searching the hall for the slender figure of Elinor. Nothing was more important to me than her good opinion and even Edmund noticed my preoccupation, chuckling quietly to himself. I responded by reddening slightly and puffing my cheeks. First love was a serious business.

That whole next year was a time of general peace for me. The Danish army had returned to York and it looked unlikely that they would venture beyond their borders for a while. They had recieved a bloody nose at Nottingham and were, in all likelyhood, nursing their injured pride and planning their revenge. We, in turn, felt confident that we were becoming ready for any threat that they might pose in the future. The meeting of the kings at Nottingham had forged some sort of agreement that they would support each other against the Danes and this tenuous alliance had been further strengthened by visits of nobles to each others courts.

Throughout that long summer Edmund's court played host to a large variety of visitors. They came from both the Mercian court and that of Wessex and although I was present at most of the official meetings, as the armour bearers were expected to be, I do not remember any of them with any real clarity. I know now that one of them was Alfred, brother to the king of Wessex, who later became king himself and led the armies that finally defeated the invaders but I have no clear memory of him. He, who I served in my time, was just another of the young noblemen who were entertained until late in the great hall. My main memory of them all is that I wished they would go to their beds at a reasonable hour so I could retire as well.

My main activities during this time, apart from the distant adoration of Elinor, consisted of a very simple routine. Most of the day was taken up with lessons and training and the evenings would be spent in the company of my father, or if he was away, the other warriors. I did see more of my father at this time. With the peace still holding he had more time to spend at home and at the court. The border patrols had been relaxed slightly, although they still happened and my father could leave much of the worrying to deputies. He was often called to council by the King and sent on missions throughout the kingdom. This was not a time of inactivity for Edmund or his warrior band for they saw it as an opportunity to train and strengthen the army. During that summer the whole army was once more assembled, although in small separate groups, and each man had to undergo training and prove his readiness to fight if need be. I enjoyed this period of slight respite, journeying regularly between my father's hall and the court, and I began to feel really at ease for the first time since the sack of the manor.

This new found feeling of happiness and self assurance must have been noted by those around me for, during that autumn and winter I noticed that the attitude of others changed towards me. I was given more responsibility and began to be treated rather as a young man than as a child. True I was fourteen years old that winter but it was still a young age to be given any real responsibility. Perhaps my now large size gave them the impression that I was older than I truly was. Whatever the reasons were I was happy to play along.

King Edmund's early life.

The early life of Edmund, who he was and where he came from, is still much of a mystery. The earliest chronicler to touch upon the subject is Abbo of Fleury writing in 985, 115 years after the death of Edmund.

His story, taken from Edmund's armour bearer via St Dunstan, is consistent with what little is known of the politics of the period. He declares Edmund to be **'a scion of a noble house among the old Saxons"** and **"descended from kings'** both of which are quite possible. The old royal house of East Anglia had been overthrown by Offa, king of Mercia, in about 794. Offa had undertaken to subdue many of his neighbouring kingdoms and his success had placed Mercia at the height of its political and military power.

Offa's might and authority increased until he was accepted as overlord by all the other Kings of Anglo-Saxon England. His most lasting memorial has survived to the present day in the form of 'Offa's Dyke', an earthwork stretching along the whole Welsh/English border. This massive bank and ditch was, until recently, thought to have been made for defensive purposes but is now accepted as having been raised to form a distinct border between the Saxon and British lands.

Offa's power was such that Charlemagne, king of the Franks, treated him on equal terms and married one of his sons to Offa's daughter. Though barbaric by reputation Offa was one of the strongest rulers England had seen since the collapse of Roman authority.

After Offa's death Mercia once more split into its constituent kingdoms as the kings of Wessex tried to unite the country. This was hampered by the ever increasing Danish raids that ravaged the coastline from Lindisfarne to Devon.

With the break up of the greater Mercian kingdom and the ever increasing Danish raids it is likely that the East Anglians looked to the remains of their old royal house to again lead them. This is where Edmund would have played his part.

Although much of this is conjectural it does tie in with Abbo's account of Edmund's lineage and also fits the political geography of the time. Had Edmund been related directly to any of the other Royal houses in England it is likely that he would appear as such in the chronicles. Strong blood ties are often mentioned and in a time when blood ties and family relationships help form natural alliances they would have been unlikely to have missed such a connection in the case of Edmund. Evidence, or lack of it, points towards Edmund being an imported king from old Saxony with possible ties to the old East Anglian royal house of King Ubba.

The Anglo-Saxon kingdoms of England, especially those on the East coast, retained close links with their older Saxon partners on the continent and although a gradual divergence had taken place over the centuries since England's conquest they were still bound by similar traditions, languages and blood ties.

Many of the later stories, including that written by Geofrey of Wells, elaborate on the lineage of Edmund, some even going so far as to name his parents, yet none of them is reliable. They also tend to give highly coloured accounts of his early reign with the possible object of making him seem marked out for sainthood at an early age. However, what they do seem to have achieved is to give Edmund the reputation of being a rather ineffectual king, too otherworldly to rule with skill. There is, however, no evidence to this effect.

The Bury tradition, dating from the time of Abbot Curteys in the fifteenth century, claims Edmund was born in 841 and was son to Alkmund and Siware. This is by no means impossible and yet there seems to be no direct evidence to give it credence.

For Edmund to have become king at such a turbulent time shows that the East Anglians either had faith in his ability or did not have the means to stop him taking power. It was common during this period for a kingdom to overthrow their ruler if they considered him less than able. The kingdom of Northumbria was in the process of overthrowing king Osbriht when the Danish army attacked in 867.

Whichever way Edmund gained the throne, and held onto it, shows that there was more to him than just a saint in the making.

The Arrival of the Danes and capture of York

The Anglo-Saxon Chronicle states that in the year 866 a **'Great heathen force'** landed in East Anglia. Here they settled for the winter and acquired horses for their coming campaign. It is also stated that **'they [the East Anglians] made their peace with them'**. From this it is unclear whether any conflict took place or whether the landing was opposed. Tradition states that in the year of the initial invasion a resistance war was fought against the invaders. Many of the stories associated with Edmund and his early miracles and escapes have been attributed to this period and yet there is no evidence for any such conflict.

It is likely that the invaders landed in the area known today as the Norfolk Broads. This area has changed a great deal since then and would have consisted of a group of sparsely populated islands and waterways surrounded for miles by rough marshland. Open to the sea at various points it was the near perfect sheltered and defensible harbour for a large body of ships.

It is unlikely that Edmund had the ability or the inclination to oppose this landing with any force. He would have had little warning of their approach and the raising of his army would have taken time. With winter approaching fast his options were limited and the best he could hope for was time to review his military position and perhaps make a little profit from horse trading.

Although not mentioned in any of the chronicles, it was common practice at the time to buy off the invaders with large qauntities of gold. This practice was not looked upon as a disgrace as it was often only seen as a method of delaying the inevitable fighting. Even the great king Alfred was not averse to a little bribery and during his epic struggles with the Danes in 871 he eventually paid a large sum to secure a peace. It must be noted that Alfred had already fought nine battles that year and buying peace was seen simply as a wise precaution.

It is equally unlikely that the Danes would have been inclined to fight. It is likely that they had gained at least some coinage from Edmund during the peace treaty and it would be unwise to spurn the chance of easy profit. East Anglia was not their main target as we see from later events and the signing of a peace treaty with the local king gave them security for a winter of preparation.

In the spring of the following year [867] the invading Danes made their intentions clear. According to the Anglo-Saxon Chronicle:

'The army went from East Anglia over the Humbers mouth to York in [the kingdom of] Northumbria. There was great discord in this people amongst themselves; they had overthrown their king'.

It appears that the Danish army arrived in York to find themselves in the midst of a civil war. The Danes took York and it was not until late in the year that the two contenders for the throne, Osbrith and Aelle, realised where the real threat lay and combined their forces against the invaders. The Chronicle continues:

'They [the Northumbrians] gathered a great army and sought the force at York, they broke into the fort; some went in and there was immeasurable

slaughter amongst the Northumbrians, some inside and some outside. The kings were both killed and the survivors made peace with the force'.

The feuding of the rival kings had come to nothing and the civil war ended with the whole kingdom under the invaders domination. The Danes undoubtably exacted a heavy payment from the surviving Northumbrian nobles in exchange for a peace treaty. For the next few years the Danes seem to have made Northumbria, and in particular York, their base of operations, campaigning during the summer months and returning to its safety with the onset of winter.

The attack on Mercia

The following year [868] the Danish force invaded Mercia, the central English kingdom that bordered both Northumbria and East Anglia. Here they captured and settled down at 'Snottingham' [now Nottingham]. The Chronicle continues:

'Burhred, king of Mercia, and his counsellors asked Aethelred, king of Wessex, and Alfred his brother [later Alfred the Great] that they help them, that they fight against the force. They went with the west saxon troops....to Nottingham, and the force met them at the fortifications. They beseiged them'.

It has been suggested by some historians that Edmund and his East Anglian troops joined the force beseiging Nottingham and, although possible, the only evidence for this is that after the Danes had retired to York, as they did with little fighting taking place, Burhred signed a charter in favour of Crowland Abbey. This took place, traditionally, at the instigation of Edmund and was signed and witnessed by Edmund and Alfred, brother to the king of Wessex. No mention is made in either the Anglo-Saxon Chronicles or Asser's Life of Alfred of Edmund of any East Anglian troops being present at the siege.

Whatever the truth of the matter it is evident that the Danes did not care to fight the combined armies of Wessex and Mercia and retired to York. It is also interesting to note that Burhred had little confidence in the ability of his army to eject the Danes from Nottingham without the help of the West Saxon troops. Even the combined strength of these two kingdoms seems to have been insufficient to ensure victory against the well fortified Danes within Nottingham. As the Chronicle relates, no heavy fighting took place and the Mercians made peace with the invaders. This no doubt involved certain large payments to the Danes once again.

During 869 the Danish army appears to have stayed within the confines of the kingdom of Northumbria. This may have been due to their setback at Nottingham and the partial failure of their attack on Mercia but it also gave them time to prepare for their next campaign - the invasion of East Anglia.

The Witness

When I awake it is always the feeling of clammy cold that stays with me the longest. The nightmare is always the same and even if the morning I awake to is bright and warm it still takes several minutes to shake off the dark musty coldness. The coldness closing above my head and my fingers scrabbling for purchase on the dank slime of the near rotten timbers.

Timber always rots in the fens. There is no way it can be stopped. I am sure that a piece of timber completly covered by tar and sealed from the damp would still rot to pieces within six months of being left in the fens. A dank, smelly, infectious place that no sane man would ever wish to live in. But live there they did, those web footed fenmen, among the marshes and eels and I never heard any of them speak of the place with anything but pride.

I can understand well enough why the monks settled there. For they were truly mad and thought of it as their penance upon earth. If they really sought a penance could they not have simply whipped themselves or starved themselves rather than subjecting their bodies to the foul airs and the pestilence it carried. Mad bastards all of them. I say that with reason for I knew many of them well and, pleasant though they were to me, they had not an ounce of sense between them. Mad with the ecstacy of their God, that's what they were, not like the rich living, soft skinned bastards that I now live amongst. At least those monks of Ely that I knew all those years ago were a hardy, honest group of men. Mad maybe, but I did have some respect for them.

I met them first in the winter after my fourteenth birthday. I had gone with my father to Ely to spend several weeks with him and his men patrolling the fen borders. I had expected excitement, all I got was tedium. I had expected night rides in pursuit of Danish spies, all I got was a sore arse from sitting on a bench in the monastery listening to my father interview travellers. I had expected hot pursuits, all I recieved was dank feet and a mild case of fen fever. In short it was a boring two weeks in which I probably got on the nerves of all in my father's command. I returned to Thetford, shivering, sweating and farting and believed that I would never again wish to go anywhere near the island in the swamp that was Ely.

The fact that I did return had little to do with free will. When the spring came the King decided that I would be of more use to him elsewhere. The fact that I had learnt that Elinor was in love with someone other than myself may have had something to do with it. I am sure that my long face can have been of little comfort to the King at a time when he had to be at his most vigorous and I was packed off back to Ely to act as a message carrier for my father.

This was a general improvement all round for I enjoyed riding and in the spring sunshine Ely did not look quite as bad as it had in the bleak wintertime. My duties were light to begin with and I spent several happy weeks riding to and from Ely with messages for my father's captains. When I had time to myself I would wander by the river or sit and talk with the older monks. I got on well with most of them and one old man in particular. He was an ancient fellow, he seemed to be many years older than even Aelfric, and he liked my company as well as I liked his. I would often seek him out by the river where he could be invariably found fishing. This was an art he taught me and although I never had the time to perfect it I did catch several reasonably sized eels.

His name was Osmund and although I knew him for only a short time and knew very little of his life I liked him greatly. Although many years have passed I still think of Osmund and our fishing together and it makes me smile. He had not always been a monk, that much I did learn, and he had spent his youth as a bird catcher deep in the marshes. He and his family had grown up on one of the hundreds of small islands that dotted the wetlands and made their living by farming the waterfowl and eel that grew in such great numbers. When he had first come to Ely as a young boy he had thought it to be the largest and finest city in the world. The monks' church dominated the crest of the shallow isle and the slopes had been covered with great halls and huts that made up the town. To me then this seemed almost laughable. Ely was a small place, full of squalid huts and drafty run down halls, the market place smelt forever of fish and there was not a stone built dwelling to be seen. The only buildings of any note were the monastery that the monks had built around the church but even these were of little consequence when compared to any single one of Edmund's holdings. I wondered what Osmund's reaction would be to a fine city such as Thetford. I liked Osmund a lot. He gave me a feeling that perhaps I was luckier than most lads my age. I had travelled, had seen sights he could only dream of and had a bright future. After only a couple of weeks I found that even Elinor, and the hurt I felt, began to receed.

I was with Osmund, fishing by the river, the afternoon that one of my father's servants came for me. This was unusual for most of my afternoons were my own but I was told that I was needed urgently. I left Osmund content by the river, staring at the dark waters, and made my way up the gentle slope that led to the monastery over a mile away.

My father had taken over one of the monks' halls as his headquarters. It was not the nicest of buildings for the monks had used it mainly for storing salt that they used to preserve the eels with. They obviously had a thriving trade for even after it was cleaned several times the smell would always return and the salt would leave a fine white powder on anything that got damp. In Ely everything was damp and soon all our clothes showed white at the edges.

When I arrived in the courtyard I could see that something important had been happening. Several of the horses had already gone and most of the rest were being saddled. The monks kept their distance but were obviously intrigued by the sudden action within their midst. I made my way into the hall to find it already full of people. My father must have summoned all those under his command that were near to hand and had also summoned some of the local wealthier townsfolk. He stood at the far end of the hall, leaning over a trestle table, and animatedly pointed to several scraps of paper that lay in front of him. I was too near the back to hear what he said but I could see that he was not pleased. Gradually some of the people left, all rushing in different directions, some to the town and others to the horses. I was called forward and my father thrust a scrap of parchment into my hands without looking up. He told me to mount up and get the message to one of his captains as quickly as I could. I was to wait for a reply then return with all speed. It was only then that he looked up and realised that it was his own son that he was speaking to. He smiled a rather wan smile and told me to be careful for the Danes were on the move and looked to be heading our way.

This was it. This was the excitement that I craved. Armies were on the march and I was bearing tidings to some of the troops who would band together and smash the heathens. I felt a lightness about me as I ran to mount the horse. I had never felt as fulfilled as I did at that moment. This joy was only slightly tempered by me then having to dismount again and return to the hall. I had, in my haste, forgotten to ask where the captain was to be found.

After riding till it was almost dark I reached the captain's camp and was disappointed to find that he was not there. Furthermore, when he returned I discovered that he had already heard the gist of my message from a rider he had met on the way. I felt almost as though I had been cheated and was determined that, instead of sensibly waiting until it was light, I would return to Ely with his message that very night. He tried to change my mind but there was little he could do. He may have been a captain of a warband but I was the son of his superior and so it was that I set out to travel the five or six miles back to Ely along little known tracks in the dead of night.

I know now that I was a fool but I was fired up with a nervous energy and would not have done any differently even if ordered to do so. There was no chance of me being able to sleep that night so I reasoned that I had best spend the time delivering the captain's reply. That is how I found myself lost and wet in the middle of the fens on what appeared to be the darkest night of the year.

I had only gone a couple of miles when the horse first threw me. A coot or some such bird startled him and I was unceremoniously tipped into a brackish pool. I managed to catch the horse easily enough and remount but it did dampen my spirits more than a little. The second time it happened I landed on solid ground. The saddle was wet from my soaking tunic and I could not grip the polished leather and so I was once more on the ground. The fall was a hard one for it knocked the wits out of me and when I came round I was alone. My head throbbed, I had lost the horse, and a grey light was beginning to show in the east. I did not know how long I had lain senseless but it must have been a good hour or more. I was still damp and the cold had left my limbs slow and aching. I clambered to my feet and tried to remember which way I was travelling. In the early grey light I could make little out and the trackway was not as obvious to the eye as it had seemed the day before. I think I must have still been dazed by the fall for instead of waiting for full light I set out in the direction I judged to be correct.

Within an hour of setting off I was hopelessly lost. I knew I was travelling in vaguely the right direction for Ely lay to the east and all I had to do was walk towards the sunrise but this is easier said than done when the land you have to cross is a marsh. Several times I had been up to my thighs in water and silt and I could now find no trace of a path. Worse than this I was feeling so very tired. I suppose it was a reaction to the blow to the head but at that time all I wished to do was curl up and go to sleep. It was like a heavy weight pressing down upon me and the effort needed to keep my eyes open was was getting greater by the minute. What I did have the sense to realise though was that if I did fall asleep then I was as good as dead. In the cold morning air, tired, wet and exhausted I would have stood no chance and would have been dead before ever I awoke. I summoned up every ounce of energy I could find and pressed on through the mire.

I plodded on for several hours but seemed to make little headway. Sleep almost overcame me whenever I stopped to rest so I had to keep moving ever onwards. The only way I could keep going was by sheer willpower and anger. I was angry at myself, at the horse, at the stupid wet stinking fen and I cursed them all loudly and probably incoherently. I let rip with every curse I could think of. Every curse I had ever heard uttered was repeated with venom to the chill morning air and I struggled onwards.

It must have been near midday when I spotted them. I had been trudging alone, eyes to the ground and feeling very sorry for myself. My anger had passed along with most of my remaining strength and I could not even make the effort to curse anymore. Besides I had long past run out of new curses and old repeated curses tend to become a little less atractive after the tenth time. I was a complete mess. My tunic was torn and wet, my leggings covered in mud up to my thighs and I had managed to lose a shoe in one of the many quagmires. I fished around for it for several minutes but to no avail and I limped forward at a greatly reduced pace.

I was clambering through a sedge bank and up a slight rise onto one of the tiny islands when I noticed them. There were a dozen or so men in a small boat rowing stealthily along a broad channel about a quarter of a mile away. I could see them quite clearly and was about to call out for their help when a thought struck me. These men neither resembled the fenmen I had seen in Ely or the warriors in my father's command. That they were warriors I had no doubt for I could see the reflected light from shield bosses and spears and so with a quicker wit than I was normally credited with I surmised that they must be Danes.

I had not been seen by the raiders as yet so I quickly retired back into the edge of the reed bank. If I could watch them while remaining hidden myself I could then make my way back to Ely with the information and my mission would not have been a complete failure. I was almost happy again. At the time I felt no fear, certain these were the first of the enemy I had seen but to me they were more of a curiosity than a threat. I remained in the reeds and watched as they drew nearer.

They were obviously trying to be as wary as I was. They made no hasty movements and tried to keep themselves as quiet and low in the water as possible. They had something to fear and every few moments one or the other of them would stretch their necks to try and see over the surrounding sedge. I followed their gaze and my heart leapt for there not more than a mile or two away was the isle of Ely rising murkily out of the fen.When I had missed my path in the night I had obviously wandered too far north and had missed the dry land by little more than a mile. I must have been travelling within sight of the northern edge of the dry ground. From this distance I could even make out the monks church on the summit. Now I was near my goal and my father would soon hear of this party of spies.

The Danes were uneasy, that was clear for all to see, for they were but few in number and were very close to one of our strongholds. How they came to be that close I did not understand. Perhaps they, like myself, had arrived under cover of darkness and with the coming of the dawn had found themselves almost within hailing distance of the town. I recognised the river they were on now as the very same that I had been fishing in with Osmund only the previous afternoon and had to stifle a little laugh as I imagined their faces when the sun had risen to illuminate their predicament. So even these fearful heathen Danes could make mistakes and look foolish. All of a sudden they did not look like the terrible army of my imagination but rather as plain men, fallible as the rest of us were. That thought, and the view of Ely across the marsh, did much to raise my spirits as I watched them pass out of sight round a bend in the river.

It still took me well over a hour to reach the outskirts of the town and by then the elation had worn off and the tiredness had returned. My feet were cut in several places and I could feel the return of the fen fever clawing its way through my bones. From the edge of the town I was met by several of my father's men who had been posted as look outs. They were not exactly pleased to see me but did bundle me on to one of their horses and lead me up to the monastery. With the sense of relief flooding over me I bagan to relax and fell asleep while astride the horse. It was only the quick reflexes of one of the men that saved me from another fall. I was in a state, sweating and shivering, and doubted that I would have made that last climb if they had not been there.

As we entered the courtyard my father came out of the hall to greet my little party. He was obviously pleased to see me again and relief was written all over his face. I was carried into the hall and sat on one of the benches against the wall. All three crouched around me asking I know not what questions. I was almost too far gone to answer anything and knew that if I did not tell my story at once then sleep would overtake me. So out it all came in one long, and probably garbled, rush. The dark ride, the fall, getting lost and finally the Danish raiders. This last part soon wiped the small amused smiles from their faces and as I fell asleep I heard my father ordering one of his captains to pursue the enemy.

It was a deep dreamless sleep, one of the most restful in my life and when I finally awoke the next morning, refreshed and hungry, all signs of the fever had disappeared. I had slept all the previous afternoon, through the night and late into the following morning and felt as though I had slumbered away a thousand years. I was still within the hall at the monastery but some kind soul, my father, I learnt later, had lifted me from the bench onto a rough mattress at the far end. From where I lay, in that dream world that is half in and half out of sleep, I could see my father and most of his captains gathered around a table at the far end of the hall. All the doors and shutters had been flung open to let in the weak spring sunshine and it made patterns on the mail that each of them wore. The fact that they were dressed for a fight was not what finally made me leave my warm blankets but rather that they were eating.

I sleepily wandered up to the table and joined them. My father made room for me and passed a beaker of ale in my direction. I attacked the bread and fish as if I had not seen food in a month and even attempted some smoked eels, a dish I normally avoided. The others took little notice of me and after a quick couple of questions my father returned to his previous conversation.

The whole setting seemed unreal somehow. The day before I had been staggering numbly through the swamp, spying on Danish warriors and generally miserable and now here I was just one day later, back with my father and his men listening to them discuss horses. I just sat there and steadily munched my way through a warm fresh loaf.

I gathered from the conversation that the men sent to find the Danes had caught up with them towards evening. The river had widened by that time and it had been impossible to come to blows with them. They had, however, exchanged spears and several of the enemy had been badly hurt if not killed. Our only misfortune was that one of the younger warriors had stood still too long taunting the enemy and had paid for his foolishness with an arrow in his arse. He was well enough but would be taking his meals standing for a week or so.

This incident had amused all the captains present and I could imagine what the young warrior would have to suffer at their hands in the years to come. I vowed never to bare my arse to the enemy unless, that is, they were well out of bow shot.

We still sat at table after the dishes had been removed and I realised that the meal had only been the prelude to one of my father's council meetings. I remained in my place and as no one seemed to object managed to hear all that was discussed. The topic was of course the Danes and what I heard disturbed me greatly.

Reports had been arriving all that morning that the Danes were at Peterborough. This was shocking news to all of us. Peterborough lay only a short distance across the fens and the heathen army could be upon us within two days. One of the captains, who had been stationed further to the west, reported that he had seen a red glow in the sky the previous night and we all assumed that the town had been put to the sword and burnt. If the Danes had taken the town the previous day then it was possible that they could be at Ely tomorrow.

My father had sent word to Edmund and had set scouts further out into the marshes. Edmund's spies had obviously had no time to send reports of the enemy's movement and we assumed, at the time, that the Mercians had been caught out by the speed of the Danes' advance. Several of the captains were confident that if we could delay the Danes at Ely it would give our army time to gather and also allow the Mercians to attack them from the rear. If we could hold Ely and the Mercians came to our aid then the Danes would be finished. My father, usually the first to think well of any man, was not at all convinced that the Mercians could be trusted. He had been brought up by his father on stories of Mercian treachery and the tyrant Offa and events in recent years had done little to change his opinion.

Nevertheless, my father did agree that if the Danes were coming our way, and reports did indicate this to be the case, then Ely must be defended. If only to give Edmund time to gather the rest of the army. So after over an hour of talking and planning, some of which I dozed through, my father sent his captains off with orders to ready their warriors and set to strengthening the defences.

When all had left the hall save ourselves he went through my story with me once again. He had been worried by my being late to return and it had obviously caused him much distress. Each was all the other had left now.

After some few minutes the Abbot was sent for. My father told the white haired old man of what he knew to be happening and suggested that if he and his brothers made haste they could be well away from the isle by the morning. He even offered to let them use some of the soldiers' horses for the old and infirm but the Abbot would have none of it. He declared that God had sent each and every one of them to that place and if they were to be attacked then God would protect them. My father replied that it would, in fact, be he and his warriors that did the protecting and that they could not guarantee the monks safety. This startled the old Abbot but he still would not be convinced, if they were to die then it was Gods will. I personally wondered how many of the other monks and townsfolk shared his resigned fatalism. It is easy to say that you are ready to die when you have already spent seventy years on this earth. I wondered how he would have felt had he been twenty.

When the Abbot finally left us my father let forth a string of curses that I would have been proud of the previous day and I mentally added them to my store for further usage. My father cursed the Abbot for a fool and said that it would make things more difficult having the town full of people. He need not have worried on that score for as word spread of the imminent Danish attack the townspeople took to the roads and flooded to the east.

I watched many of them leave that very afternoon. My father and I had, after seeking the Abbot's permission, climbed the tower of the church to get a view of the town's defences. The Abbot had been busy supervising the burial of all the monastery's valuables in the small vegetable plot that lay behind the church and had simply waved a dismissive hand in response to my father's polite request. From the top of the tower we could make out most of the town and beyond onto the isle proper. The road that led to the east was dotted with groups of people, pack ponies, oxen and carts all heading for safety and a strange sight they made carrying all of their possessions and valuables on their backs. Whole families were simply closing up their houses, grabbing all that was portable and leaving the town to its fate. I could not really blame them for what we could make out of the defences did not exactly inspire confidence.

Both the earthen rampart and the timber palisade that topped it appeared to be in a poor state of repair. Little had been done to them in recent years for when the English kingdoms fought each other religious settlement were usually left in peace. Mercia had been Christian for over a century and Ely did not fear destruction from them. The Danes showed no such respect for holy places and although my father's men had repaired small stretches of the walls they were in a sorry state. Even from this distance I could make out areas where the earthbank had been eroded away and the timbers of the wall leaned at alarming angles. My father had never had the men to spend too much time upon repairs. We knew then that we would pay dearly for this oversight.

Later that same afternoon my father and I rode the full length of the defences. He had concentrated all the effort of the day on repairing and strengthening the walls that lay to the west for he reasoned that if the Danes did come then that was the way they would approach from. The actual town of Ely stood at the eastern end of the isle and so gained valuable protection in that direction from the marshes. If the Danes came they would approach from the western end, where they could come dry shod, and hopefully, seeing the walls newly repaired and well defended would be content with laying a siege rather than risk an all out assault against the walls. If they came from any other direction then we would have been as well to mount the horses straight away and run for our lives.

Do not think me cowardly for saying that we were prepared to run from the Danes. That was my father's intention from the beginning. Ely was no place to defeat the invaders but it was a good place to slow them down and if we could gain Edmund a few days then our time would not have been wasted. We did not intend to waste our lives in a fight that we knew we could not win. Every soldier in the garrison was ready to run with the best of them if the need arose.

That night as darkness fell my father and I joined most of the other warriors back in the monastery. We had left sections to patrol the walls and had lookouts posted well forward as a precaution but we did not expect anything to happen until the end of the next day. We all ate in the courtyard of the monastery and built fires around which groups of warriors huddled. From the small church came the sound of the monks at their devotions and I know that many of the warriors joined them at some point or other.

It was a disturbing night, that night before the attack, no one seemed to sleep much although everyone was quiet and subdued. The fires sent strange shadows leaping up the walls of the church and everyone was content to merely sit and watch the night out. A few conversations were carried out in hushed whispers and occasionally a snore would grate its way through the dulled night air. I remember feeling how calm it all was. There seemed to be a feeling of great peace hanging over us all and even I was eventually lulled into a dream infested slumber.

I was awoken with a start just after dawn. Some clumsy fool with a great red beard had managed to stand on my hand as he attempted to climb over me to get into the hall. When I had fallen asleep I had been sitting upright against the carved doorjamb, covered in my blanket, and I had somehow managed to slip sideways in the night to block the whole doorway. Judging by the number of sleeping figures left in the yard and by the murmur of voices coming from within the hall I reasoned that half the warriors in the garrison had already had to step over my sleeping form that morning. In the early dim light of what was going to be a sunny day I was suprised that no one else had trodden on me before the redbeard. I got up and finding myself stiff and aching went to break my fast with those in the hall.

We spent that morning much as we had spent the previous day. Groups of warriors were sent into the fen to watch for the Danes while the remainder continued work on the defences. My father reasoned that I could be of little help to either group, he did not want me lost again and I had not the strength to work the great timbers, so I was set a task all to myself.

With the departure of most of the townsfolk the market was no longer operating and food was difficult to buy. If we were to be sieged then we would need a good store of all sorts of things and so I was sent off into the town to see what I could find. My father had given me permission to break into any of the properties that were closed up and see if there was anything of use that had been left behind. I was also furnished with a bag of coins with which to pay any of the residents who would sell us food. This was of less appeal to me than the housebreaking and so I decided to concentrate my efforts in that direction.

To tell the truth I spent an extremely happy morning, one of the most enjoyable in all my young days. It was an adventure all in itself. The first house I chose to investigate was only a little way down the hill and looked as though it would provide rich pickings. It was a large hall set back in a walled yard that had a high timber wall around it. Several outbuildings butted against the wall and it was only a matter of moments before I was over the barred gates and in the yard. I was halfway across the yard when the two dogs appeared.

Great brutes of animals they were, all hair and teeth. They came shooting out of one of the outbuildings, teeth bared and looking ready to kill. I turned and ran, only just beating them to the gates which I leapt at. The bar gave way and I was deposited neatly in the middle of a pile of horseshit that lay in the road. I did not even think of this at the time but rather curled into a ball expecting to be savaged at any moment. I could hear the ferocious barking loud in my ears and waited for the first bite that would signal my end. It never came.

When I gathered enough courage to finally look up I saw that both dogs had stopped at the open gateway. They both still snarled and barked at me but neither would cross the threshold. The stupid animals could have ripped me apart there and then but they had been so used to not going beyong the barrier that even when it no longer physically stopped them they would not pass it. I picked myself up and quickly made my way further down the street.

The incident with the dogs annoyed me all that morning. I entered several other houses and halls and had a great deal of fun searching through the property of the missing owners but my mind kept going back to the hall with the dogs. I had actually found quite a lot of provisions that had been left behind and each item was placed in the street so that the returning guards could pick them up on the way back to the monastery. The one item I hung on to was a large ham that had been left in the rafters above a fire to be smoked. It was a very fine piece of meat and I had great plans for it.

Towards noon I started my journey back up the hill. Most of the goods I had ransacked had already disapeared but I still kept my ham clutched to my breast. I reasoned that the hall with the dogs was one of the finest in the town and that the owner had left the dogs there for a purpose and that purpose was to keep the likes of me out. If they wanted to keep me out then they obviously had left a great deal behind worth protecting. If they wanted to keep me out then I wanted to get in.

When I reached the hall it was much as I had left it. The gates were swung outwards at an odd angle and the two dogs lay on the threshold. At my approach they both got up and started to bark with all their might but once again they would not cross the threshold. I simply walked up to within a few feet of them and sat myself down in the road, this time avoiding the horse shit. I then took out my small knife that hung from my belt and started to carve away at the joint of ham. This did not stop their barking but it did diminish slightly. When I had cut up the whole joint I spread it around me on the road. I then simply threw a few of the smaller scraps at them which they swallowed almost without tasting and moved to the side where I hid behind one of the gates.

With my disappearance the barking gradually ceased and it was replaced by a snuffling sound. The larger of the two was edging towards the scattered pieces of ham and the second dog was not far behind. In under a minute both dogs had edged their way forward and were greedily swallowing large lumps of the pink flesh. It was then a simple matter of running around the gate and pulling both closed behind me.

The howls of outrage that followed this manoeuvre were really something to hear. I am sure that my father must have heard them and wondered what I was about but they very quickly died to a rather pathetic whine. Now the dogs were the wrong side of the gates they were not sure what they should be doing. Soon both were lying down, noses pressed against the gate timbers whining to be let in. Feeling very pleased with myself I went to investigate the hall.

It took me no longer than a few minutes to break in. The doors were well and truly fastened but I managed to force one of the wooden shutters and climbed in to the gloomy interior. The hall was large with a cement floor and as I opened more of the shutters I could see why visitors had been made to feel unwelcome. The whole building was much as it would have looked normally with virtually everything still in place. The residents had obviously decided to leave only at the last moment and had taken almost nothing with them leaving the place with a feeling that they had just left to go to the market and would return at any moment.

I searched the whole building and found a large supply of food that would serve most of the garrison for at least one whole meal. This I transported out into the yard and placed on the roof of one of the outbuildings next to the stockade. From there I could easily retrieve it without having to enter the yard. I had tricked the dogs once and did not favour my chances of repeating the performance.

When I had removed all that I thought would be of use to my father I returned to the hall for a last rummage around. I did this more out of curiosity than anything else for I was in no rush to return to the monastery. All within the hall was of a fine quality and spoke of the wealth of the owners, from the decorative hangings that covered the walls to the carved and ornamented benches. I viewed everything with a detached interest for although items of this quality were nothing new to me, I had seen such objects everyday within the King's hall, it was the first time that I had bothered to look closely at the craftmanship involved. One object I kept returning to again and again.

Hung on one of the end walls was a fine shield. The iron boss had been polished to a high shine and the painted leather had been given a coat of fine beeswax so that it too glowed in the dim interior of the hall. I had seen many shields before, all the warriors carried them, but this was probably the best I had come across. It was not decorated in any ornate manner, simply a design of lines and dots in red and black, but the whole piece gave off a feeling of quality. I longed to own such a shield as that but knew that just taking it would be going beyond what my father had ordered. I tried to ignore it but always my gaze would be drawn back to the polished circle on the wall. Eventually I could stand it no longer and took it down from its hooks and that was when its true quality became apparent. It was so light. The whole was easily as thick as any of the shields of my father's war band but it weighed only about half as much. The moment I held it I knew that it must be mine.

I withdrew the purse of money that my father had given me from the breast of my tunic and hung it on one of the hooks that the shield had been on. This was not stealing as far as I was concerned but a fair bargain. There was more than enough money in the purse to buy a normal shield five times over and I considered this shield well worth it. Of course it was not my money that I was paying with but I had collected a great many supplies and how was my father to know that I had not paid for any of it. I thought this bargain to be more than fair to all the parties involved.

And so with my new shield slung over my back I started to make my way up the hill to the monastery. Firstly I climbed onto the top of the wall by the gates and let the dogs back into the yard. They appeared more than pleased with this and slunk off back to their kennels. I then closed the gates and hopped down into the road taking with me as much of the food as I could carry.

When I arrived back at the fishy smelling hall that was our headquarters I found my father in a rather sour mood. He seemed well pleased with my haul, which now covered several tables, and told me I had done well. He did eye my new shield but made no comment upon it even when two of his captains spoke of it with admiration. My father thought that the town was likely to be destroyed anyway and so any item that could be of use was fair game. Already that morning he had ordered several houses to be pulled down so that the timbers could be used to strengthen the walls. He had also had a timber barrier constructed at the bottom of the sloping hill that led west from the monastery. If the walls were breached too quickly then the barricade would serve to slow the enemy down and the narrow street could be defended by a handful of warriors.

Although the town was a little better able to defend itself than it had been a few days previously my father was less than confident. His sour mood had been caused by the loss of two of his scouts to a Danish spy boat travelling up the river. This boat, possibly the same one I had seen, had caught the scouts unawares and by the time the noise of fighting had drawn others to their aid it

61

was too late. They were both found dead upon the riverbank and the Danish boat was withdrawing quickly downstream.

The bodies of the two men had been carried to the monastery for burial and already the monks were busy digging the graves, determined that any who died in their defence would be buried in the monastery graveyard. Muttered voices from among the silent band of warriors who watched commented that the monks had better dig a bloody great hole if we were all to fit in.

I watched with the others as the two bodies were lowered into the ground and as the second blanket-wrapped corpse was lifted to the edge of the pit the hastily wrapped cloth fell aside to reveal the face. There, staring at the blue sky with unblinking eyes, was the red-bearded face of the clumsy warrior who had woken me that morning.

I did not know his name, or at least if I did I have now forgotten it along with so many other things, but I felt strangely saddened by his death. His was the first body I had seen since the raid that had killed my mother and to see death so close once again brought much of the pain back to me. The death of my mother, my nurse, my friends and now the red-bearded man were all caused by the same people and this struck something deep within me. It was not fear or even anger but rather just a determination that they would pay for their crimes. Pay for our lives with their own. This new found resolution had its chance to be tested before the sun had set that evening.

The first we knew of the approach of the main Danish force was when a rider came trotting into the courtyard at the monastery. We had heard his approach and were all in the yard to meet him. He did not bother to dismount but simply reported to my father that a large body of men had been seen moving along the isle from Sutton way. Smoke could be seen further to the west and several families had fled to our defences to escape the advancing force.

It was still only mid afternoon and the Danes were marching fast. They would be at the walls in less than two hours the messenger believed. My father wasted no time and, sending the messenger back to his post, called for all his captains to make ready. I did not really know what to do. I had been assigned to no one group and so thought it best to stay close to my father. He returned to the hall with me in tow and started to don his war gear. I followed suit and grabbed my new shield and spear. It was the same one that Aelfric had given me and although I had replaced the shaft several times as I grew larger I had always attempted to polish it to be as good and bright as the day it was given to me. With my shining shield and polished spear I must have appeared on of the best equipped warriors in Ely.

I must say I did not feel so well equipped. I knew that it was unlikely that I would end up face to face with an axe wielding Dane but still I felt unprepared. All the long hours of practice and mock combat really amounted to very little when one's fighting for life. I felt no real fear, but I did feel nervous. I was more worried about disgracing my father than getting hurt. I knew my weaknesses and felt that they would appear obvious to even the most inexperienced Dane. All I could hope to do was follow my father's lead and try not to either make a fool of myself or end the day in the grave pit.

They say it is only a fool who does not feel fear before a battle and I can truly say that before the fight at Ely I felt no fear. Oh, I have felt it enough times since to recognize it but that day I did not really know what lay in store for me. What lay in store for us all. I suppose I must have been a fool.

From the hall I followed my father up to the top of the church tower. We already had lookouts posted there and they would shout down occasional reports but I guess that my father wished to see everything for himself. The view from the top was quite spectacular. Based on the top of the hill as it was the whole of the town and surrounding countryside was laid out at our feet. To the west smoke still rose from what must have been the site of villages and we could just make out groups of men approaching from the west. It was not as I had expected, a great dark mass of warriors moving as one, but rather lots of smaller groups spread out across the whole width of the isle. The only thing that even betrayed that they were warriors was the occasional metallic glint as the sun caught a spear, axe or shield boss. To me, at that distance, they could very well have been small herds of cattle grazing their way forward across the landscape. One of the lookout commented that they looked like nothing more than a mass of hungry dung beetles all heading straight for the manure pile that was Ely. A mild enough joke but in our tense and strained moods it caused much laughter. My father had seen enough and we returned to the ground.

We stayed in the courtyard for the next hour or so. I wandering aimlessly around its borders while my father issued orders to the constant stream of warriors that passed back and forth through the gates. Reports would be yelled down from the tower and all was silence as we stretched our ears to catch each word. With each new report my father would issue fresh commands and instructions and send men running to the ramparts with his orders. As the afternoon progressed we could all of us see that things were not going to go as planned.

The Danish scouts had already found to their cost that the walls were held against them in strength. A few wounded were beginning to trickle up the hill from the walls and the occasional cry or scream could be heard on the light afternoon breeze. The monks had set up one of the other halls as a surgery and the minor wounds were treated quickly and the warriors returned to the walls. We were told that their had been no deaths on our side as yet but the Danish scouts were using their bows well and most men on the walls were keeping their heads down.

What worried my father was the fact that once the scouts had found their way blocked they had not retired to the main body of their army. He feared that their recent victories had made them so confident that they would not lay a siege of any kind but rather wait for the main force to arrive and then assault the walls without delay. In our present situation they would sweep all before them and even if we caused them many losses it would still be as a gnat bite to a horse. Annoying but of no consequence.

There were still several hours of daylight left when the lookout reported that the main Danish army was within bow shot of the defences and looked to be making themselves ready to attack. My father climbed the tower one last time to see for himself exactly where the main brunt of the attack would be borne. When he returned to ground level his face showed the anxiety that he felt within. The Danes were preparing to assault a weak section of our defences and my father, barking forth a final set of orders, set off down the hill to oversee the defence in person. I followed a few steps behind fearful that I would be sent back to the monastery. I need not have worried overmuch for my fathers mind was occupied with far weightier matters.

When we arrived at the defences I could see the reasons for my father's concern. The section that was under threat was one of the oldest part of the town's defences. It was built much as the rest, a timber wall running along a raised mound with a ditch on the outside, but it had seen little attention in the years before we had arrived. True, we had replaced some of the most rotten timbers and shored up what we had no time to deal with but it was really the ditch and earthen bank that was the problem. My father had pointed out its defects the previous day on our tour of inspection. The height around most of Ely, from the base of the ditch to the top of the earth bank, was some nine or ten feet but here the bank had been eroded by heavy rain and filled in some of the ditch with as much as a foot of soil. This had left great dark gashes in the bank which would serve any attacking force as footholds and had also made the base of the ditch drier than the areas to either side.

The whole of the weakened frontage covered no more than seventy or eighty feet but our warriors were spread very thinly around the whole of the western wall. My father had sent additional warriors to this area but as they crouched behind the timber wall, avoiding the arrows of the sharp eyed Danes, they looked very few in number. This fact was only made more apparent when I managed a quick glance over the timbers of the wall.

I realise now that the horde of warriors I saw facing us that day was only one section of the whole invading army. This advance force wished to take the town and all it held for themselves before the rest of the force arrived and wanted it done quickly. To me, however, it was the most formidable sight I had ever seen. There must have been well near a thousand of them standing almost shield to shield. They formed a dense block about two hundred feet away from the wall with what seemed hundreds of archers covering the ground between. I felt more impressed than scared for an army in battle order is a sight to behold. Standards flew above the mass, sun glinted on spears and some shouted and leaped before their comrades, wearing little more than wolf and bear skins. They still held back and I could see that more groups were joining them as the minutes ticked by.

Their archers were beginning to be a real problem. The shafts flew over and into the walls with a regular soft thudding sound. They realised that we had few bowmen with which to respond and as long as they stayed out of spear range they were safe. Gradually they began to creep closer and closer to the wall.

Occasionally, one of our warriors, out of curiosity or bravado, would raise his head above the wall to look at the enemy. This action would be met with a hail of arrows as the warrior wisely ducked down with some haste. I only saw one man who was not quick enough to respond and he paid for his slowness with a shaft through one of his eyes. I did not actually see him hit but just heard a soft gruff grunt as he fell backwards. I turned around in time to watch him hit the floor, the arrow still sticking proudly upwards. He was dead before he hit the ground. This small victory caused a ragged cheer to rise from some of the nearby Danes and an angry muttering in response from our men. One of our archers found a gap between two rotten timbers and felled one of their archers with a shaft in the throat. This time our warriors gave the cheer.

The whole thing began to take on an unreal quality for me. Was this warfare? Our warriors crouched behind the wall muttering alternate curses and jokes. Their army standing at a polite distance laughing, waving and capering. It seemed more of an elaborate and occasionally fatal game than a battle. Then, just when I had began to laugh and joke along with the rest, the arrows stopped.

The warriors babble stopped almost as one and brave souls began to peer over the wall. The archers were scrambling back to their lines. Our men stood up, adjusting shields and belts ready for the onslaught that was to come. I looked at the sky, surely there could be only an hour's light left at best. I joined my father at the wall and was just in time to watch the Danes begin their advance.

They came slowly at first. The whole mass moving forward as one. Then they began to trot and pick up speed. The ground was quickly eaten up and the gap between us shrank. Our warriors stood silently watching the incoming wave with never a glance to either side. How could we stop such a force? I felt they would simply wash over us barely pausing in their stride. The first of the enemy were close now, speeding onwards, their rush headlong and unstoppable. I gripped my shield tighter and peered round the mail-clad bulk that was my father. But then, just as I expected the force to crash into the stockade at full pelt and take all with it, they began to falter.

Those out in front obviously realised that to reach the wall alone and in front was unwise to say the very least. Their charge began to slow as they waited for the solid comfort of their comrades and they reached the edge of the ditch at little more than a fast walking pace. Of course a few had been less sensible and had almost thrown themselves at the wall but they were dealt with in a matter of seconds. I watched, fascinated, as one young Dane leapt towards my father's left, his spear raised high. The next moment he was being casually cast off the end of three spears to slump into the ditch beneath him. He did not make a sound and I was put in mind of the way in which the eels were stuck with the eel spears to be casually lifted to the bank.

The main body attacked in a mass. It was slow and almost calculated. A spear flashing out only to be deftly turned aside. An axe wheeling downwards into a shield. Sharp points of steel thrusting forward, feeling for soft flesh. Withdrawing and thrusting again. Screams where metal met flesh and the disgusting sound of butchers' slabs.

We did lose some men in that first attack. I watched horrified as a spear came plunging through a gap in the planks to pierce the belly of a warrior. Quickly withdrawn it was followed by a dark fountain of blood. The warrior collapsed in screaming agony trying to hold his guts in place as his life bled out between his fingers. An axe took another in the face, his whole head seeming to explode in a red mass. Others, mainly with head wounds, clumsily retiring from the fight.

We may have taken some injuries but it was as nothing compared to those suffered by the Danes. We had the wall to hide behind and had the advantage of height. Many of our warriors were leaning well over the edge hacking forever downwards into the screaming, bleeding mass below the wall. When they withdrew a few yards, as they did after five or ten minutes, the ditch was full of the dead and dying. They must have lost five men for every one of ours. Yet this did not deter them. After a few minutes regaining their breath they again started their shouting and screaming and on they came again. Back to the dying.

This is how the fight continued until the sun finally settled down into the horizon. Short five minute scrambles of blood, screams and pain before retiring to regain strength and breath. It was during the third or fourth assault that I killed a man.

I had kept fairly well out of the way up until that point, somewhat behind and to my father's right, but during that desperate struggle the Danes came near to breaching the wall. They were pressing up close and we were being pushed backwards and I found myself thrusting away Danish spears from my father's flank. I had just pushed aside two blades and we were moving forward when a great hairy Dane with plaits in his beard leapt forward to thrust at my father. His head was thrown backwards and he was screaming incoherently as he leapt at the wall. My spear was resting atop the timber and I simply thrust forward.

It was no very great lunge but he had been watching my father and not me and the blade caught him full in the throat. His own weight drove the blade in deep and I saw the flesh ripped away as he began to fall. Blood flooded out of the wound and down the spears shaft. As he dropped below the line of the wall the blade slashed itself free out out the side of his neck sending up a little shower of red droplets. I had killed the man without even thinking about it. So stunned was I that my father had to push me backwards out of harm's way. I again took up my position behind him and tried to wipe the memory from my mind.

That was the worst of the Dane's assaults that evening and gradually as the twilight mercifully obscured the mess in the ditch the Danes retreated to a safe distance. We stood, not knowing what was to come, and assessing the damage. It was only when we saw fires being lit that we realised that it was over for the night and began to relax.

We had suffered badly, nowhere near as badly as the enemy, but badly enough. They had the men available to replace those that had fallen, we had not. Throughout the fight my father had called for extra men to be sent from other parts of the wall but he dared not weaken any one section too much for fear of a separate attack. Our ranks were thinner than an hour previously. We had over a dozen dead, mainly from head wounds, and over twice that many hurt. My father had been cut in the arm by a Danish sword and now squatted down to tie a cloth around it.

I knelt at my father's side trying to help him but my fingers shook too much and I could not fasten the knot tightly enough. My father laughed at this and called another over to help me. I simply sat next to him, exhausted and numb, watching the Danish fires and absent-mindedly trying to wipe the blood from my spear.

In my mind that night is a blur. I remember eating, but what the food was or where it came from I cannot tell you. I was so tired that I slept curled up at the base of the wall not even bothering to find a covering. The night was full of fires and voices but none of them seemed to make any sense. There were several alarms and I stood again at the wall, staring into the blackness, but nothing happened. In my dreams I killed the Dane again and again.

I awoke to the sound of distant screams. All around me warriors were leaping up as fast as their weary bodies would allow. My father was already standing, shield and spear in hand, shouting orders to messengers and peering into the darkness to the north of us. Shouts and screams echoed through the night and I began to realize that they were coming from further along the wall. The Danes were attacking another section of our defences. A section that must surely have been sparsely defended as reserves had been sent to strengthen our section.

We set out at a trot, about half of us, following my father and the sound of conflict. It all had a dreamlike quality, jogging through the night in search of the source of the shouting. We came across several warriors trailing back from the walls, blood seeping from various wounds, and my father questioned them urgently. The Danes were inside the walls. They had broken through before the guards had a chance to even yell much of a warning.

We reached the place of the attack after what seemed like forever stumbling through the darkened streets. The sound carried on the night air and the fight was much further away than I had first guessed. The Danes had broken through but they had got little further. As we approached the wall up one of the narrow streets we could see that the whole mouth of the road was blocked with a struggling mass of men.

The enemy had breached the wall at a place where it stood only a few yards from the buildings to either side of the street. Now they had no more room to fight than we did and their extra numbers counted for little. If they wished to advance then it had to be down the street itself and that was now blocked by our men who we quickly reinforced.

It was a bloody sharp fight in the darkness of which I saw very little. I was behind the main mass of warriors and could make out very little except that it seemed a desperate struggle. A few warriors would stagger past me clutching at some wound or other but even these were mercifully obscured by the darkness.

We were holding the entrance to the road but we paid a heavy price for it. More and more of our warriors fell or withdrew hurt from the fight and it looked as though it would only be a matter of time before we were overcome. What finally decided our fate was the fires.

67

The Danes had managed to get some of their men into the yards behind the houses where they fought desperatly bloody scirmishes with some of our men. It must have been difficult for both sides for the yards were cluttered and full of hazards for unwary feet. No one cared for the idea of stumbling into a shit pit in the dark. The enemy had tried to get behind our line through these yards but had found their way barred and so they had taken the drastic action of setting fire to the thatch.

Even after a sunny day the thatch was still damp but gradually the fires took a hold and soon the whole scene was lit by an orange glow. The heat was building up and my father knew we would have to retire very soon. He shouted at me to run the length of the walls to the south and tell the others to retire to the barricade below the monastery. I set off back down the street as fast as I could without even a glance behind me.

How I managed that run I will never know for I still carried both shield and spear and had had but little sleep after an exhausting day. It was past midnight now and I was sprinting along to carry my father's message to all his captains I could find. They all took the news of the retreat calmly enough and set to preparing to fall back. Not all the Danes had been involved in the assault and now other stretches of wall seemed to be under threat. The captains knew that they had to be organized in their withdrawal or face a bloodbath.

When I finally reached the furthest point of our outposts I simply turned around and started to run back to the monastery. My legs were like lead, my muscles ached and my breath only came in short gasps but still I sprinted for all I was worth. I wanted to be at the barricade when my father retired there. I knew it would not be easy for him to fall back and keep his men in order and so wished to make sure that the barrier was well manned to support him.

When I arrived the first of the other troops were already in position. The barricade was stoutly made and was a more formidable obstacle than the outer wall with a narrow frontage that made defence easy. Some warriors and our few archers had been placed in the yards of the halls to either side of the road and from there they would attack the exposed flanks of the enemy as they crushed into the narrow street. We all stood silent, save for the sound of my panting, and listened for the sound of my father's approach.

We could hear the sounds of battle coming closer by the minute. Several groups had been sent forward to aid the retreat and we could see fires springing up in other parts of the town. The Danes had well and truly breached the walls and now it was just a question of getting my father and his men to safety. The shouts and screams grew louder 'til we knew that they were just out of sight around the curve of the street. And then all at once the noise grew less.

The street ahead was almost completely dark and it showed as a slightly paler strip against the black bulk of the building. All of a sudden it was full of running figures. My father's men had finally broken and they rushed to the safety of the barricade.

All was confusion. It was near impossible to distinguish between friend and foe. Men clambered over the barricade, some to be cut down and others to be hauled to safety. Some fell under the axes and spears of the Danes as they tried to scramble to safety while a few struggling knots of brave souls tried to fight their way backwards. A few of these groups made it but most were simply cut to pieces by the overwhelming numbers of the Danes. I thought that I saw my father among their number but could make little out in the darkness. And then the Danes were upon us all.

They hit the barricade with the force of a falling oak. No easing back as they had done before when attacking the outer wall. This time they knew we were beaten and just wished to finish us quickly. The barricade stood for perhaps half a minute. By the time it finally toppled backwards the Danes to its immediate front were already dead. The sheer weight of numbers pushing behind them made it impossible for the bodies to fall to the ground and it looked as though the barricade was being toppled by a line of bloody rag dolls. When the timber hit the street and the bodies piled on top of it the Danes let out an ear shattering scream and flooded over the remains of their dead comrades. Now there was nothing to stop them and we ran.

I ran with the best of them. My heart pounded, my lungs hurt and still I ran. I ran past the monastery yelling incoherent warnings at the shocked looking monks who appeared at the gateway. I glanced back in time to see the first of them spitted on a Danish spear. I ran onwards. I could hear others behind me but didn't know whether they were Danes or not and did not dare to look again to find out. I ran down towards the river shedding spear and shield in my haste to escape. My vision blurred and still I ran. I was no longer even thinking about anything. All I wanted was to get away. To run from the Danes. To run from the blood. To run from from the bloody mess that was once Ely.

I came upon the river almost suddenly. It lay before me, a great black band barring my path. I simply ran until I had no ground to run on and plunged into the cold black water. The cold of the water hit me like a fist in the stomach. I surfaced and struck out for the other bank, my arms wearily crawling across the wide expanse. I gasped for breath, saw other figures in the water, my tired limbs almost failing me. It became hard to breathe and I was confused. I seemed to be swimming forever. The bank was invisible and I was exhausted. I felt that I was getting nowhere and would never reached the other side. I thought I was going to die. The sheer stupidity of it all struck me, to fight a Danish army and then die by drowning. I was almost crying and laughing at the same time. The end was near. Soon I would not be able to keep moving and then I would die.

My hand struck something slimy and hard. My stroke was lost and I started to sink, the cold black water closing silently above my head. I opened my mouth to scream and felt the chill water start to fill my lungs. I struck out wildly. My hand again struck something hard. I scrabbled at it and felt the slimy wood of a post driven into the river bed. I grabbed at it and hauled my way upwards. Upwards out of the stinking water. My face broke the surface and I clung to the post greedily gulping in the night air. Then I was sick.

Retching and spluttering I held onto my post and tried to get my bearings. Gradually it dawned on me that I was almost at the other bank, it stood as a blck line only a few yards away. I gingerly felt for the river bottom with my feet. I could just feel the soft mud and knew I could make the final short distance. I took time getting my breath back and tried to take in all that was happening around me. There were others in the water and I could make out the dark shapes of figures that had managed to haul themselves up the other bank. No one was speaking and all that could be heard was the occasional bout of coughing and retching. Even those that sank out of sight into the cold river made no outcry, they were simply too exhausted to even scream.

I managed the last few yards with relative ease and scrambled my way up the bank where I lay cold and still panting. Others were around me but no one seemed to have the energy to even check on their comrades. We just sat or lay stretched out and watched the death of Ely happening on the other side of the river.

The fires had spread and new ones had been set. The flames were reflected in the once again still waters of the river and made the whole scene appear even more unreal. The monastery and church were now alight, flames shooting high into the night sky as the tower acted as one great chimney, occasional bursts of sparks and flames would leap upwards as a roof collapsed inwards. We heard a scream echo across the river.

Gradually the sky in the east started to show paler where the dawn was preparing to make an appearance and the ragged, unarmed band that was once my father's command began to stir. Slowly and stiffly getting to our feet we stared walking towards the promised sunrise, turning our backs on the burning town, and prepared to return to our King.

The East Anglian campaign of 870

Of the Dane's campaign of 870 that resulted in the capture of East Anglia the Anglo-Saxon Chronicle has little to say:

'The force went over Mercia to East Anglia, and took winter quarters at Thetford. In that year, St. Edmund the king fought against them 'atrociter' [all out] and the Danes took the victory, killed the king, and overcame all the land. They destroyed all the churches they came to; the same time they came to Peterborough, they burned and broke, killed the Abbot and the monks, and all that they found there. They made that which was very great such that it became nothing'.

But from this scant amount of information, and what we know of Anglo-Saxon warfare in general, it is possible to reconstruct many of the military events surrounding Edmund's defeat. Within this short passage is contained much that sheds light upon the Danes' movements and from these we can anticipate the likely military response which would have been undertaken by Edmund.

The first thing of note mentioned in the Chronicle is that the Danes 'went over Mercia'. This indicates that, as at Nottingham two years previously, the Danes were a land based force rather than water borne. It is known that they acquired horses during their first winter in England and although they were almost never mounted in battle, they were used extensively for transport. The horses would be used to carry troops and supplies to a battlefield, but once there, the troops dismounted and fought on foot in the traditional manner.

This land based force is said to have crossed Mercia and, as no fighting is said to have taken place in the process, it may be assumed that either the peace declared at Nottingham in 868 still held or that the Mercians had little time to react to the sudden march of the Danes and could raise no troops in time to engage them. The probable route used by the Danes was through eastern Mercia crossing the Humber by boat and moving down Ermine street, the old Roman road that is now roughly followed by the A15.

The old Roman roads were no doubt still in use in the ninth century and although likely to be poor condition they offered one of the few methods of transporting large bodies of troops from place to place. Unlike the Roman roads the Saxon roads tended to be less of a system of trunk communication and more of a haphazard method of connecting one market town with another. Where possible the Saxons transported large quantities of goods by water and although not averse to using the old Roman roads they seem to have had no policy of maintaining them.[9]

It is interesting to note that when the Danes began to settle, after the peace of Wedmore in 878, of their five strongholds, or 'Burgs', four were situated on Roman roads.

By using the Roman road the Danes could travel quickly south to the junction with the fen causeway near Peterborough. It is here that they began their destructive campaign and made it **'such that it became nothing'**. From this point the fens and East Anglia lay before them.

The Fenland of the ninth century would have been very different from the flat open agricultural plain that we see today. It was a marshland, criss-crossed by causeways with the villages set amidst the wetlands. These few meagre habitations were built upon the natural mineral islands and their size was regulated by the amount of dry land available. The Romans had been the first to attempt to drain parts of the fens and even constructed a new town in the marshes, but as with most other Roman projects this had all been abandoned and left to decay four hundred years previously. The fenland marshes acted as a natural defence on East Anglia's western flank and like the similarly sparsely populated areas on the west coast of Ireland they had become the home of religious communities seeking solitude and isolation. From Peterborough there are two main routes east across the fens. The first is across the northern fens following the old Roman causeway north of March to arrive on the high ground at Denver, just south of Downham Market. This route must have appeared the less attractive method of crossing as it seems the Danes favoured the slightly longer southern route.[10]

Unlike the northern route the southern road was not a single causeway but a series of short, raised dykes linking the natural mineral islands that were the usual sites of Anglo-Saxon settlements. This southern route began by travelling from Peterborough down Cnut's causeway to Ramsey, the site of a second Abbey ravaged by the Danes. From there it travelled east past the early British fort at Earith and onto the Isle of Ely. Here the Danes once again destroyed the religious community and then continued along the Stuntney causeway, destroying the settlement at Soham before regaining the high ground just to the north of Newmarket.

It is also likely that the invaders had boats moving down from Northumbria in support of their main land force. Abbo of Fleury's account even suggests that the whole army came by sea. In similar attacks made on the south coast it is known for an army to have landed and then moved around the countryside keeping in touch with the naval force. In the case of the East Anglian campaign it would have been a great advantage for the Danes to have had at least some longships available and finds in the fens themselves indicate that there were navigable waterways which would accommodate the shallow Danish craft. One apocryphal story relating to the Danes in the Fens states that in the eighteenth century, during a long hard winter, a certain village discovered an entire longship buried in the peat soil. The village had been cut off by severe weather for many weeks and so by the time spring arrived all that remained was an entry in the parish register commenting that the ship kept them warm all winter.

The Danes managed to cross the fens destroying all that stood in their path and carrying off their treasures. By this time it is probable that Edmund had news of the Danish advance and was gathering his forces somewhere in East Anglia.

The Witness

We walked for several hours. I was so tired that I hardly remember any of it. I was concentrating on putting one foot in front of the other and that was enough for any of us. Who directed us I do not remember for my father was, as far as I was concerned, dead. Someone must still have been thinking clearly though for by a couple of hours after dawn we found ourselves at Soham.

Even at the best of times I thought very little of that stinking rat hole but that morning it looked particularly bloody. The people had, for the most part, fled. They had seen the flames of Ely and heard the stories of the Danes and so followed the example set by the inhabitants of that blackened town. A few did remain and they were kind to us. They fed us and gave us blankets and even some horses but they did not want us to linger long in their blighted settlement. They reasoned that if we were there when the Danes arrived, as they surely would, then it would go badly for them. We were not strong enough to defend them and so they wanted us gone.

It was at Soham that we came across my father once again. The monks had a settlement on the outskirts of the village and it was there that we went in search of help for our wounded. Several of the soldiers had been hurt in the flight from Ely and the river crossing and walk through the cold morning had done little to help their condition. We arrived at the monastery to find a dozen or so soldiers there before us. They were of a different breed to the warriors I was with and appeared almost of a different race. Where we were ragged, unarmed and exhausted they stood proud and steadfast, their battered shields still gripped fast.

They were the remains of the group my father had led from the desperate defence of the barricade and they had fought every inch of their way out of the shattered town. My father led them still, very slightly wounded and exhausted but still the proud warrior I remembered. His arm was deeply cut from an spear thrust but the monks had bound it with clean linen and in exchange he had given them one of his golden bracelets that the king had honoured him with. He greeted me with a great shout and a hug that almost broke my ribs before he set to reforming and re-arming the dispirited group that I had arrived with. After several hours of care and attention we once more began to resemble a war band. Spears and shields had been found and now over half our warriors were armed once more. With the return of arms came a renewed vigour and confidence that almost made us forget our losses.

Of the war band that my father had led into Ely in the spring less than half now remained. True, we had no idea how many had escaped in other directions but it seemed unlikely that many more had lived through the running battle that was Ely. I had seen dozens fall myself and when this was added to the number whom we knew to have fallen before the Danes breached the wall it made a sorry story. Had these been the raised militia men of the local levy then it would not have mattered so much but these were the best and proudest troops that East Anglia had at its command. The battle at Ely could not really have ended in any other way but it was still a blow to Edmund's forces, even if Edmund did not know of it yet.

We set off from the monastery in the middle of the afternoon and passing a deserted manor holding struck out to the east. We had acquired a few horses that helped the wounded and generally speeded our progress but we were still an exhausted little group. To stay that night in Soham would not only have endangered the inhabitants but ourselves as well, so we pushed on as far as we could before the light failed and we had to stop for the night.

Luckily we found a manor that would take us in for the night and as the last light sank to the west we ate what little food we had and curled up to sleep the night through. My father stood guard for the first hours of the night and as I lay down to rest I remember seeing his dark bulk leaning against the outer gate, staring to the west.

We were woken early next morning by the arrival of one of Edmund's messengers. He had been as far as Soham and the outskirts of Ely and, not finding us there, had followed our trail to this manor. What had happened to us was obvious but the messenger, an associate of my father, was delighted to see that so many of us had survived. When he had initially approached Ely, and been accosted by Danish patrols, he had feared that we had been all but wiped out. His search had been only for a few straggling survivors not a well ordered war band.

His joy at finding us gave heart to the whole band and we exchanged news and gossip avidly as we hurriedly broke our fast. Edmund, he said, would know of our fight by now and be preparing his own defences. Several of my father's messengers had got through and Edmund had sent forth groups of scouts to keep him informed of the enemies' movements. The Danes appeared to have settled at Ely for the time being and were probably licking their wounds and sending out scouts in much the same fashion as ourselves. The whole army was to muster upon Thetford as soon as may be and we were to make our way there keeping a wary eye open for Danish warbands along the way.

The messenger left us soon after the meal, his fine horse showing in stark contast to our poor ill-kempt ponies as he rode through the gateway. He raised a hand in salute to my father, and promised that we would all meet again shortly in Thetford, before kicking in his heels and cantering away to the East.

My father decided that we could best spend the remainder of the morning by resting and preparing for the march. Now he knew that most of the Danes were still in Ely he felt the immediate threat was not great and that we could take time to gather ourselves in safety. A few guards were posted and a couple of horsemen sent out to scan the route we would have to take but other than these few measures we were all left much to our own devices.

I spent the morning in the hall with the family who owned the holding. They were pleasant company and I enjoyed my time retelling, and probably exaggerating, the story of the fight at Ely. It was pleasant in the smoky hall and as I spun stories for the younger members of the household, of which there seemed to be a great number, I remember thinking that this is how I would like to spend my old age. I could now see how attractive Aelfric's lifestyle was and I felt a pang of guilt at the small lies I was telling the children. Aelfric had a lifetimes,adventures to expand upon yet I made my small expedition sound almost as fabulous.

One of my enchanted listeners especially caught my attention. She was a fine looking girl of about my own age, perhaps a year or so older, and although not officially part of my audience she somehow managed to always be within earshot. What ever she was about within the hall, be it spinning, soothing a crying youngster or attending the fire, I could see that she always had an ear open for my tales. It disturbed me a little for she kept glancing in my direction with a slight grin curling the corner of her mouth. I feared she realised my story was not all as truthful as it might have been and was finding amusement at my expense.

Her presence made me feel a little uncomfortable. She was an attractive young woman and I was at the age where I was most interested and most unnerved by such interest. Her glances came to be met with a returning glance from myself, an act I happily noticed brought forth a sudden blushing redness to her cheeks.

My self congratulation was brought to a sudden and final end by my father. The order was given for us to prepare to leave and after a hasty and confusing half hour we were all assembled and ready to march. We left the manor about midday, I with many a backward glance, and made our way west.

Within an hour of leaving the manor we came across trouble. Our road was running through a slight defile in between low, gently sloping hills when we spotted a small band of warriors away to our left. My father sent a horseman to investigate, expecting them to be levies for Edmund's army, and was wholly suprised when, after ten minutes or so, the report came back that they were Danes.

We outnumbered the raiders by perhaps as much as three to one but my father still thought it best to ignore them and press on with our journey. We had more warriors, it is true, but not all were armed and many were injured and so notwithstanding the grumbles among the warriors we carried on eastwards. The Danes were moving faster than we were and would soon be well out of sight and my father believed his actions to have been sensible in the circumstances.

The Danes obviously had different ideas. They were waiting for us along the edge of a small woodland about a mile ahead. We could not believe it was the same group for they must have been out of their wits to take on such a large group. We discovered afterwards that most of the Danes were drunk at the time, senseless from stolen spirits and ale, and that they would probably have attacked an entire army as quickly as they did us. When ale is in, wit is out, as my mother used to say.

The fight was short and very bloody. Only about half our warriors were involved, the rest of us standing to the rear cheering them on, and it was good to see the Danes recieving some of which they had given at Ely.

They advanced at a trot in a very loose formation, shields waving and shouts of defiance issuing from their throats. The shouts were soon turned to screams as they hit the tight line made by my father's men. They were lightly armed, few had mail shirts and not all wore helmets, but they advanced as fearlessly as any hearthguard. Their ale-fuddled heads made them slow and they were soon pushed into a tight knot of struggling men as our line closed around them. More of our warriors joined the fray as they snatched up the weapons of the fallen Danes and soon there was little to see except the backs of our men and the rise and fall of axes and swords as they slashed downwards into the ever decreasing circle. I watched with grim satisfaction.

Few of them escaped the slaughter and when the circle final broke up and drew back, with only one dead and a few minor wounded, we had left a great bloody heap of twisted offal by the edge of the woods. What the crows and ravens made of it I'll never know but they had been left a rare feast.

We took what we could from the dead, not an act of shame for most of it was probably stolen from English manors, and soon most of our men who were fit enough to fight had something to fight with. The dead man, a soldier I did not really know but friendly enough, was buried with some haste and my father said a prayer over him before our small column moved off once more.

It took us all the next and most of the following day to reach Thetford. We acquired more horses along the way and this made the going much easier but still it was a trial for all of us. We were all tired and weary and it was only the thought of warm dry beds that kept us moving at a good pace. We saw very little of any Danish activity and save for a few distant scouting parties, obviously more sober than their fellows, felt ourselves almost alone in the landscape. We crossed the bleak inhospitable breckland and then followed the river until we came within sight of the town.

It was then that we realised that all our fight had not been in vain for Edmund had used the extra time to his advantage. The whole town was transformed and even from the distance it was clear that a great army was being mustered. Horses stood grazing in great paddocks all around the walls and where before fields had been now stood new villages of tents. Armed men were everywhere and wherever we went they cheered us. We made our way to the King's hall with high spirits and good humour.

What we found within the King's holding put us in a slightly less jovial mood. My father had dismissed those men who had family or friends within the town and so we numbered less than two dozen when we finally entered the stableyard. Grooms quickly ran to grab at bridles and the rest of the men sent to eat and rest while my father, his captains and I went in search of the King.

We found him in the main hall and obviously furious. Somehow a Danish messenger had overtaken us on our return trip and his message had been delivered to Edmund shortly before our arrival. The Danes had offered him his life, kingdom and people's freedom if he would become a subject king of the Danes. They also wished for all the royal treasury and land for those warriors that wanted to settle. Edmund felt it was a personal insult. The Danes considered him beaten already and he would have none of it. The messenger had been sent back to the army with a sharp reply and a small bag of coins which they were told to spend wisely for that was the only gold that they would get from Edmund.

Our arrival did lighten his mood somewhat. He was pleased that we had survived with so many warriors and he even spared a few words for me alone. I could tell that he was still out of sorts but his knack for treating people well soon had me almost back to my old self. A few minutes of solemn greetings and conversation and I was sent to my bed to rest. The captains stayed behind to talk with the King.

Relieved as I was at returning home and tired from the journey and its alarms and diversions I fell asleep almost as soon as I lay down on my bed. Fully clothed as I was, I slept through the whole evening and night without a murmur. Even the roisting return of my fellow armour bearers late that evening did nothing more than make me turn in my sleep.

I was woken by a sharp kick in the thigh early the next morning. The sun was barely risen and one of the other lads, clumsily searching for some previously discarded article, managed to almost trip over me. I could make out the figure of the steward in the doorway, come to summon the other two for some duty or other, and made to rise myself. The steward, not normally the caring type, waved a hand in my direction and told me to lay still. I would not be needed until later and should gain what rest I could for, he said, things were as busy for everyone here as they had been on the march. I sleepily mumbled my thanks and soon fell into another slumber.

When I awoke for the second time the sun was high in the sky. I had no exacting tasks to perform and felt safe and secure in my bed so just lay for a while watching the shadows in the thatch roof. How long I lay I cannot tell, for it was a superb feeling, lying dry snug and warm with hardly a care in the world. Now we were back in Thetford it would surely only be a matter of days before our growing army was supplemented with the first arrivals from the armies of Wessex and Mercia. When joined we would turn on the Danes and smash them to pieces, sending their scattered remains back to the north if not back across the sea. How long had the Danes left? A week, perhaps a fortnight at most. They could destroy a lot of holdings and villages in that time. I felt a trace of concern for the pretty girl and her family on their manor near Soham. Our revenge on the Danes would be great as it was but if anything happened to her I promised myself my own revenge. My safe and ambitious thoughts were finally interrupted by the entry into the small hut of Elinor.

She entered the dark little hut almost stealthily, obviously thinking me still asleep, and her figure showed lithe and elegant against the square of bright gold that was the door. She approached the bed slowly, almost on tip toe, for her eyes could make out little in the dark after the brightness of the morning sunlight. I made a move to get up but stopped quickly, suddenly realising that I was naked beneath my blankets. The other lads must have taken pity on me the night before, or perhaps they just thought it a great joke. I heard Elinor whisper my name and I whispered hers in reply. What came next was completely unexpected.

77

Elinor rushed the last few paces to my side and knelt by the bed. She kept repeating my name again and again, anguish and relief showing in her trembling voice. Her arms encircled my neck and before I knew what she was about she was kissing me passionately and, it must be said, rather clumsily, full on the mouth.

This coming so soon on top of all the other shocks of the previous week proved almost too much for me. My head felt light and the blood was pounding in my ears. I had not felt such as this since the first attack on the wall at Ely. My arms went around her waist and I returned the kiss as best I knew how to.

The urgency in her kiss soon abated and she settled into my shoulder, a deep sigh escaping her lips. I had no idea what was going on. Never before had Elinor shown the slightest interest in me. I had always adored her, so had most of the young lads about court, but she only had eyes for another. It had been one of the reasons that I had been sent with my father to Ely. Confused as I was I still had the sense to recognize a good thing when I saw it. As I lay with Elinor in my arms, mind reeling and confusion abounding, I said not a word.

After a few minutes she rose to leave, explaining that she had sneaked away without permission to see me, and had to return before she was missed. I muttered a few endearments, receiving another kiss in return, and then she was gone, back out into the sunlight. I was still no wiser as to what had created the change in her and did not even care to ask. The important fact was that the change had taken place. I lay still upon my bed and contemplated the possibilities that the future now held.

I rose after a short while, too excited and alive to ever consider sleeping again. I doubted I would sleep that night and I now just wished to be about the world, wallowing in its wonders. I dressed quickly, broke my fast in the kitchens and reported myself to the steward, grinning the whole time no doubt.

To my surprise there was little for me to do. The steward told me that the King and most of the hearthguard were out inspecting the newly raised troops and would not be expected back until after noon. The other armour bearers were with him, as was my father, and I should just try and make myself useful until their return. Slightly disappointed at the lack of heroic tasks left for me to undertake I went to help in the stables.

I always enjoyed working in the stables. My love of riding was accompanied by a genuine liking for horses and I was never happier than when helping out in the royal stables. The stableboys showed me the respect I thought I deserved and horses can always tell a person who likes them. The place was always warm and there was always someone about with whom one could have a good gossip.

This day the stables were full to capacity. So many horses had been gathered in for the army's use that several of the storehouses had been converted to act as temporary stables. I was in my element. Many of the new arrivals were of the finest quality and I enjoyed looking them all over and discussing their various merits with the grooms and stableboys. My quiet peace was interrupted by the unexpected arrival of Aelfric.

The old man entered the stableyard leading a fine grey pony and a tall roan. He looked tired, most of the grooms looked fit to drop, but his eyes lit up and his face broke into a wide grin as I approached him across the yard.

For the first time in my life we greeted each other as equals. Not as we usually did, with Aelfric giving his devoted follower a playful cuff round the head, but as warriors, clasping each other by the forearm. Whether Aelfric had already heard about my killing at Ely or whether he had just sensed a change in me I do not know, but we now looked at each other as brother warriors. Well almost.

I, for my part, still felt a bit of a fraud. True I had faced my first battle and even killed at least one of the enemy but I felt that neither event had really been of my doing. I had been thrown into the fray and had just been swept along by the events. Even killing the Dane with the forked beard was almost an accident. My new found status as a promising warrior sat rather awkwardly on my still young shoulders.

None of this seemed to matter a bit to Aelfric. Passing over his charges to one of the grooms he dragged me off to one of the benches by the great hall and demanded that I tell him every detail of the fight at Ely. We sat companionably side by side, sharing a mug of the steward's best mead, while I went through the story once more.

I did not exaggerate the tale quite as I had done before. I felt that Aelfric would have already heard the bare bones of the story and any embroidery on my part would look foolish but he insisted that I told him every detail. If I skipped a bit of the story or brushed only lightly across some scene or other he would interrupt and get me to retell every detail. When I came to the night of the assault he sat motionless, staring into my face, taking in every single word.

To think back on it now, that was probably the only time I have ever told that tale completely honestly, except for now that is. Every other time I have added sections or removed pieces that were unflattering and generally added to my own, or my comrades' glory. It probably did me good for when my tale was finished, and the mug drained, Aelfric merely turned to me and nodded. A good start for a story, he told me. And he was right. To see the honest truth before me, as I had laid it out for my old friend, made me feel almost at ease with the events that I had passed through without so much as a scratch when other, better men, had fallen to the Danish axes. After that day I did not dream again of the face of the fork-bearded Dane.

We were still sitting thus, side by side, when the King returned to the manor. We had finished discussing the fall of Ely and had moved on to other subjects. Subjects that, for my part, included rather a lot about Elinor and, for Aelfric's part, rather a lot about Elinor's nurse. We had tried to discuss the war in general but had avoided the subject when we realised that we did not share the same views. Aelfric did not share my confidence in the Mercians while I viewed his distrust of our allies as merely the bias caused by a long memory. As it turned out the kings arrival brought news that proved Aelfric to be once more correct.

The king swept into the main courtyard by way of the stableyard surrounded by a group of his personal hearthguard. My father was amongst them and they came striding quickly towards the door of the hall. Aelfric and I jumped up from our bench, conveniently knocking the empty mug into the shadows beneath it, and made our hasty reverences to our lord. Edmund acknowledged us both with a rather distracted nod and indicated that we should follow him into the hall. Doing as bidden I joined my fellow armour bearers behind the group and Aelfric fell into step behind us.

The hall was dark and smoky after the brilliance of the afternoon sun and the mead had made me sluggish so it was only the restraining hand of Aelfric on my shoulder that stopped me walking straight into the back of the hearthguard when they came to a sudden halt. Edmund, instead of taking his usual place at the top of the hall, had stopped at the lower end where tables and benches were still set up from the midday meal. Sitting quickly at the nearest bench he gestured for all of us to gather round the table and join him. A servant was sent running and within a few moments great jugs of ale and platters of bread and meat were laid before us all.

The King dove straight into the food, grabbing a beaker of ale as if he had not drunk in a week. The others all followed suit and only Aelfric and I, who had both already eaten, hung back. None of them had had any refreshment since dawn and for several minutes the only sound within the hall was that of vigorous eating. I made sufficient with a small beaker of watered ale.

When the platters and jugs were as near empty as they were ever going to get the servants deftly removed them and, on the Kings command, withdrew out of earshot. Then, and only then, did Edmund speak. To my surprise his first comment was to Aelfric. He asked upon the condition and training of the newest batch of troops that had arrived that morning. I had not realised before but Aelfric's views on the state of the war were better informed than I had believed. The King had, probably upon my fathers advice, made Aelfric responsible for assessing all the levy troops as they arrived, finding their weaknesses and suggesting possible action that could be taken to improve matters.

Aelfric's answer to the King was less than optimistic. He said that the troops had benefited from the training given in previous years but still were sorely lacking in quality arms and basic supplies. Another of the hearth guard interjected that he had parties out as far afield as Elmham scouring the countryside but there was little to be had. Food was not a great problem at the moment but in two or three weeks it would soon become so.

The King did not seem overly concerned with this matter, brushing it aside with a wave of the hand and slight grin, and returned to questioning Aelfric about the levy troops. Would they fight? Surely, with all their hearts, Aelfric replied. How many bowmen were there? Not enough, came the reply. Did we have time to train the levy in larger formations? Aelfric returned a sour grimace.

All this talk was unnerving me more than a little. I had thought us more than ready to beat the Danes and now I began to realise that not all was as I had imagined. Edmund was worried and if that was so then he must have good reason. In my agitated mood, and I'm sure the mead played a part, I blurted out "What about the Mercians?".

All was silence around the table. All eyes fixed on me. I received a sharp blow to the ankle from one of the other armour bearers. Edmund simply raised his eyes to mine and let out a huge sigh. His voice was quiet in the still hall and I could only just make out his words. He told me that they were not coming and neither was the army of Wessex. The Mercians had bought a peace with the invaders and the army of Wessex was far to the south defending the coast from more Danish raiders. We could expect no immediate help from anyone. We were on our own.

As the hall was once more plunged into silence I stood as a man turned to stone. I could hardly believe what I had just been told. Edmund still looking at me could see the effect his words had and at once tried to lighten the situation. He declared that with noble young armour bearers such as his he needed no extra help to beat of a rabble of pirates. Was it not true that a lad of fourteen years could kill the bravest of the Danes? The hall dissolved into laughter. The tension was gone and I grinned happily along with the rest of them.

Later, when I returned to my hut with the other two lads, I got the whole story from them. The Mercians had flatly refused us aid, which came as no suprise to some, and had said that they could not break a God sworn oath even to help their countrymen. This had been received with the contempt that it deserved for the Danes were still partly heathen and so an oath to them counted for nothing, besides the Mercians had never been noticably averse to oath breaking in the past. The King of Wessex, on the other hand, had sent messages of support and even some coin to help pay for extra troops. He had troubles on his own coast and would come to our aid as soon as he could but did not think many of his troops would be available for at least a month or more. A month seemed like an eternity away and even my father, ever the optimist, doubted that the Danes would hold off for such a time. We were going to have to fight and we were going to have to fight alone.

The next morning we were all about the manor early. Edmund was determined that he would take another trip around the ever growing camp that formed his army. I was to take the place of one of the other armour bearers that morning for, as the steward had said, they were almost exhausted. Edmund was never a man to spare any who served him. He was always the first to set an example and expected as much of his household men.

As I kicked my heels wandering around the damp stableyard Edmund was within the hall taking council with the Bishop and his closest advisors. I had learnt from the servants in the kitchen, where I had grabbed a crust and beaker of ale shortly after dawn, that the king had been up and at his business for several hours before ever I stirred from my bed. The Bishop had ridden in during the night with his own troops and the steward had been told to wake the King as soon as he made his appearance. What they were discussing was beyond the mere gossip of servants but all about the manor could hazard a fairly accurate guess as to its nature.

The Danish invasion was more than just a threat to the King and his people, it also posed a very real threat to the continued existence of the church in East Anglia. If the Danes were victorious then the Bishop and all his clerics could expect about the same treatment that would be handed out to Edmund. At best harsh treatment under a new regime and at worst, well, none of us cared to think of that. Edmund had always been a true and devout supporter of the church and, although no model Christian, he cared deeply about its future. The support of the Bishop at such a time added more than just physical comfort to his army.

It was almost a full hour after dawn when the Bishop's group emerged into the weak, drizzle laden light, and they were quick to mount their horses and leave the manor. I sympathized with them for I was still fairly dry and did not relish them their journey. I secretly hoped that Edmund would think better of his planned inspection and stay within the warmth of the hall until the sun drove the rain away. My wishing proved fruitless and Edmund's party followed the Bishop's party some ten minutes later. I shrugged my cloak about my shoulders and prepared to get wet with the rest.

Our small party consisted of Edmund, a half dozen of the hearthguard, Aelfric, another armour bearer and myself and we were soon mounted and trailing out of the gates in the stockade. The drizzle had begun to ease a little and a patch of sky showed lighter than the rest where the sun was trying to force its way through. Already it was getting warmer and in my damp clothes I felt uncomfortably clammy. Edmund and his hearth guard had forsworn their mail armour that morning in favour of thick woolen cloaks and it was not long before the first of these was removed and rolled up to be fastened to their saddles. We walked the horses slowly along the high road that led towards the town of Thetford itself and it appeared out of the misty dampness just at the moment when the sun made its first appearance of the day.

There, set out before us, was the whole town. The smoke was rising steadily from hundreds of cooking fires and, combined with the mist that now began to rise from the damp fields, it gave the impression that the scene was not real. All had a blurred edge, made more unworldly by the presence of so many tents surrounding the stockade. To me it looked like a jumble of canvas and timber that reminded me of a ship I had seen wrecked off the coast several summers earlier. The hard lines of the stockade were lost to the eye and all order seemed to be missing. As we approached the first lines of tents and crude shelters this impression was heightened by the large numbers of men who wandered from tent to tent. How was it possible that there could be any order amongst such chaos?

True, I had seen an army camped before, but never in such numbers and never so close to a town. The combination of animals, warriors, women and children gave the whole area more of a holiday atmosphere than that of an armed camp. Pedlars wandered between the gossiping soldiery, women stood by the stockade staring after their loved ones, children played with the many scavenging dogs that wandered at will through the open gates and we seemed to be all but ignored.

As the King made his way towards the nearest gate some of the officers must have recognized him for orders started to be shouted forth. All around us suddenly the camp became animated. Men rushed for their arms, the dogs scattered and the sudden movement caused a line of horses, tethered to a post, to shy away and pull free. The escaping animals, and the anarchy of their subsequent recapture, only succeeded in adding to the state of confusion.

Edmund pulled his mount up before the gateway and surveyed the scene around him. A great sigh broke forth from his chest and he gently shook his head. Aelfric stiffened beside me. He obviously expected a rebuke for the sorry state the camp was in. Edmund, on the other hand, had no such thing in mind. As a stray horse bolted ahead of us, through the open gate to be followed by a pack of snapping hounds and howling children, the gentle sound of laughter came back to us from the King. He was finding the whole spectacle as amusing as the women who watched and giggled from the ramparts.

The rest of the inspection was carried out in the same light-hearted mood it had begun in. We rode through the separate camps watching confusion and chaos spread before us like a wave. Wherever we stopped we would find something to amuse us. A tent collapsing as the warriors rushed out to greet the King. A member of the hearthguard stepping backwards into a cooking pot to avoid a loose horse. A pair of dogs happily copulating in the middle of camp, unaware to their royal viewer. All sent to amuse.

At the end of the tour, it must be said, I for one had had a thoroughly good time. I suppose that it relieved the tension of all those in the camp. The King was wandering amongst them giggling and laughing with the best of them and if he could find things to laugh at then, they reasoned, all must be well. I can see now that Edmund's laughter was as much a show and facade as was his optimism. His army, though large was under equipped, under trained and generally ill ordered. There did seem to be a lot of them but they bore little resemblance to the professional warriors I had been with at Ely.

This fact was more clearly demonstrated later that afternoon when we stopped to watch some weapons practice in a meadow outside the camp. Most of the levy men were of a poor standard and although probably deft enough with plough or oxen they left a little to be desired as warriors. They were keen enough, that was not a problem, but they did lack the practice of the professionals. So poor were some of them that even I rated my chances against them.

This was, of course, not the case with all the troops in the army. We watched some of the hearthguard at practice later that same afternoon and they told a completly different tale. Skilled and precise their mock combats sent a shiver down my spine just watching them. They were the elite of the army, the backbone around which the rest of the troops would form and although small in number, less than three hundred, they were a formidable force. Edmund had supplemented the hearthguard with a hundred or so paid men from Essex and I pitied the Danes who came up against their sleek blades.

We returned to the royal manor an hour or so before sunset, tired and saddle sore, but quietly confident. Our army may not have been made up of the finest warriors in the world but at least some were present and the rest made up for in spirit what they lacked in skill. We would give a good account of ourselves.

After handing over our respective mounts to the grooms we all followed along behind Edmund into the great hall to eat a hasty meal and discuss the day's events. I anticipated it being much the same as the day before and longed to get it over with quickly so I could go off in search of Elinor, but it was not to be so.

In the hall we found three messengers awaiting our return. They had arrived only shortly before us otherwise they would have set out to find us in the camp and all three carried serious tidings for the King. Rather than seeing them in private the King listened to their reports as we all sat down to eat. The contents of their messages turned the ale to vinegar in my mouth and I had trouble swallowing. The Danes were marching.

All three messages were very similar in content and varied only slightly in their urgency. The Danes had left Ely, or at least a large party of them had, and travelled along the causeway to Soham. Most of the locals who had not already fled did so at their approach but the monks, as before at Ely, had been slaughtered to a man. The monks at Soham had been kind to all of us who had fled the bloody conflict at Ely and I said up a small prayer for their souls as I listened with sinking heart to the rest of the messages.

The last sightings of the Danes had been as some of their scouts reached the edge of the fen and the high ground at Fordham and crossed the river Snail. Our scouts were still shadowing them and more reports were probably on the way. Edmund took the news in silence. He knew, as all of us did, that once on the high ground the Danes were virtually sitting astride the Icknield way, the main road south-west from Thetford, and that they could make good time covering the remaining score of miles to our capital.

For a large army, cluttered by baggage and loot, the trip would still be a slow one, but we could expect the invaders to be knocking on our gates, if Thetford were the target, in two days time. This was hardly time enough to mobilise what troops we had gathered let alone raise more. The Danes had to be slowed in their advance.

Edmund dismissed the messengers and turned to face his captains. His face betrayed little emotion but he knew what had to be done. There were only two sites between Thetford and the Danish army that lent themselves to defence. Both sites were fords where the Icknield Way crossed the the rivers Kennet and Lark and we would have to send a small force to defend at least one of these river crossings. The Kennet was nearer the Danes than us and so it would have to be the Lark.

My father stepped forward and volunteered himself and his men for the job. The King smiled but shook his head. My father, he said, was both brave and noble but both he and his men had done enough to prove themselves at Ely. They should let someone else have a share of the fighting. Several of the other captains stepped forward, all asking for the commission, and Edmund selected two of them. They immediately left to round up their men and Edmund seated himself glumly at one of the tables.

He knew it was fairly unlikely that he would see either man again and I think that it was at that moment that kingship weighed most heavily upon his shoulders. To lead men into battle was one thing but to calmly ask for volunteers for a mission that would probably end in death was a completely different matter. True, he had little choice in the matter, but I saw the drawn look on his face and the heavy set of his shoulders and at that moment I felt more sorry for Edmund than for either of the two doomed captains.

After some few moments Edmund had recovered himself enough to start issuing orders. The army was to be brought to readiness and concentrate its forces the next day. So far the troops were spread over a four or even five mile area, camped in small groups so as not to deplete the stores and water supply of any one area. From the main camp outside Thetford they spread along trackways and paths out in all directions and it was now time to bring them all together. By the next evening most would be with the main force and the rest only a short distance away.

Orders having been sent forth, Edmund began to discuss with the remaining captains where he should meet the Danes in force. The Icknield Way ran almost directly south-west from Thetford, in a straight line to the crossing on the river Lark. If this was the way the Danes were to come then it must be somewhere along that line of approach that they must be stopped.

The discussion carried on late into the evening. Everyone had their own ideas as to where the battle should be fought and tried to explain their reasoning to the King. Edmund sat there, listening to all of them in turn, nodding occasionally, but committing himself to no plan as yet. I remember only a few of the ideas but I do remember that most of them involved the slight range of hills that surrounded the town. Some thought we should withdraw to the north, sacrifice Thetford, and then fall on the invaders when they were busy killing and looting. Others believed we should march south, down the Icknield Way and catch the Danes unawares, but most believed we should simply take up a defensive position around the town and wait for the attack.

This last plan of action seemed to be the favourite with Edmund. It meant we would not have to leave a garrison in the town or leave it to the same fate as Ely and if need be we would be able to fall back behind the defences of the town itself.

In the end Edmund decided upon a compromise plan. The army would form just to the south west of the town on a slight rise. This small hill, if hill is not too strong a term for it, straddled the Icknield Way and overlooked both the town and a shallow valley through which the Danes would have to approach. I see now that it was not a great place to defend but I have known worse since. The river curled around our left flank, the town lay behind us and a valley to the right and front. Not a bad place considering.

85

By the time all this was finally decided I was too tired to really take it all in. I had been in the saddle most of the day, had little to eat and was now almost asleep on my feet. With the break up of the meeting I recieved a gruff, offhand goodnight from my father and retired to my bed to sleep soundly until dawn.

The next day was a busy one. Messengers tavelled back and forth between the King's hall and the camps from dawn onwards. We also received messages from the force sent to Lackford and from lookouts posted to the west and south and so the stableyard and hall had more of a feeling of a grim carnival or market day than of a headquarters. I was busy in my own right and so had little time to take any particular notice of any one thing. I did manage to snatch a few minutes with Elinor though.

We met in my small hut shortly after midday. I had been sent to change into my finest tunic for the Bishop was expected for the meal that afternoon and if he brought no servitor with him it would be my job, as the youngest of the King's shieldbearers, to wait upon him. I discovered Elinor there before me, hurriedly searching along the clothing pole, for she too had to play the servant that afternoon. She was as pleased to see me as she had been before and kissed me soundly as soon as she realised we were alone. She was changing into her best gown and so wore only her shift. Her kiss was long and lingering and I could feel the warm softness of her body beneath the bleached linen as she leant against me. My ears were deaf to her words, my senses being fully absorbed with her other beauties, and before I had time to utter more than a few clumsy endearments she was gone again. Still straightening her clothing she fled from the gloomy hut to attend upon her mistress. Little did I know it but that was the last time we ever saw each other to speak to.

As the saints would have it, I was not called to serve at the meal that afternoon for the meal never took place. Shortly after the arrival of the Bishop and his party, he had brought no servants to my disgust, a messenger cantered into the stable yard. I was just going to attend on the Bishop but was brought up short, halfway across the yard, by the state of the rider who had arrived. His horse was obviously exhausted and from the sweaty state of both horse and rider I concluded that both had ridden hard over quite a distance. The roads had dried out sufficiently for dust to be raised by the passage of a horseman and the mount was caked in fine pale powder. Dark streaks ran down the horses flanks where sweat had washed away the dust and the whole had the overall effect of making the poor beast look as though its hide bore stripes. The rider was in a similar state and, as he was led into the hall, I noticed that his hand bore a fresh bandage which showed dark where blood soaked through.

I followed into the hall in time to catch most of the message that was being delivered by the rider. He was one of the warriors sent to delay the Danes at Lackford and had been sent back to the King, his hand preventing him from holding a shield, to report on all that had happened at the ford.

The Danes had not crossed the river as yet but it was only a matter of time before they would sweep us from the bank. They had made several assaults that had been repulsed with heavy losses for the invaders but had also killed over a dozen of our best men. I watched Edmund's face cloud as he listened in silence to the continuing report. Our warriors had now retired slightly from the ford and now lay behind the old ramparts that stood a bare hundred yards north of the river. The ford was an old defensive position dating from times when our kingdom fought the other English kindoms and, although the ramparts were in poor repair, they would slow the Danes' advance still further. The messenger reported that they would hold them till dusk at least, for it would take that long for the main Danish army to reach the ford, but come the dawn there was little hope of holding their ground for more than an hour, two at the most.

This news was a suprise to us all. We had not expected an attack on the ford until the next day at the earliest and it had been hoped that we could hold the river crossing for most of the day. Now it seemed likely that the invaders would be within striking distance of Thetford itself by early the next afternoon. Everything suddenly took on a new urgency. I was sent to ride into Thetford and spread the news within the walls of the imminent danger, while others were sent off to warn the warrior bands that they must act with all speed and gather at the chosen spot south of the town. I was one of the first to leave the holding, having one of the simplest messages, and I remember looking back over my shoulder at all the hustle and bustle of the courtyard and wondering if anything would ever be the same again. It had taken me, a rather spoilt young brat, long enough to find a place that I was comfortable with and now, just as I was settled and the future held some distinctly interesting possibilities, I felt that it was all slipping through my fingers. A feeling of almost helpless anger overwhelmed me and I determined that I would do as much as possible to end the Danes' threat to my new found happiness. They had taken so much from me. My mother, my nurse and my childhood home. Now I was once again begining to feel as though I had a place in the world and they had returned once more to strip that away from me. Well this time I was ready to fight back.

That night I lay in my father's hall at Thetford. The holding and town was full of warriors preparing for the slaughter that would come the next day. As I lay sleeplessly waiting for the dawn I wondered how many of the soldiers and men I had come to know so well would look out upon the rising sun for the last time. How many of us would live until the sunset and how many would greet the next day from cold dead eyes.

East Anglia's response

It is not known exactly where Edmund gathered his army together, but in most areas there were traditional sites for such gatherings; places that had some feature that set them aside from the ordinary. The site used by Alfred, in his campaign of 878, was 'Ecbrihtestan' [edge-brights stone] on the borders of Hampshire and Berkshire and appears to have been the established site for the mustering of the troops of those counties. The mustering point in East Anglia was likely to have been a similarly central point traditionally used for the purpose.

One possible candidate for the main mustering point in East Anglia is Thetford. During the ninth century Thetford was of considerable importance, being one of the seats of the kings of East Anglia. The Saxon town was then situated on the Suffolk side of the confluence of the rivers Thet and Little Ouse, and was also on the route of the Icknield Way. This Stone Age trade route linking East Anglia with South Western Britain has been a major route through East Anglia since prehistoric times and was in regular use until recent centuries.

Anglo-Saxon Thetford itself is one of the few townships of the period to have been excavated so we have a relatively large amount of information about it. Built as a possible trade centre on the south bank of the Little Ouse it was enclosed by earthwork defences, topped with a wooden palisade and contained buildings of up to 36 metres (39 yards) in length. These buildings were of a sophisticated nature and two contained cellars while one of the excavated examples even boasted a mortared floor. There was no apparent alignment of buildings or street plan and so it would appear to have grown up casually with no formal planning. Yet from the evidence produced by the excavations it was obviously a wealthy and comfortable township.

By the time of The Domesday survey two centuries later it has been calculated that Thetford had a population of approximately 4000 and was the defensive, administrative and economic centre for a large area. Although ninth century Thetford is unlikely to have been this large it was obviously a major settlement and it is therefore not unreasonable to suppose that it might have been the site of the gathering point of the army.

Five miles to the east of Thetford on the Little Ouse lies a second possible mustering point at the river crossing at Knettishall. Here the Peddars Way and a north south Roman road both cross the river within half a mile of each other, while half a mile to the north east lies the Devils Dyke, a large and possibly defensive earthwork. Although this site offers no evidence of major Anglo-Saxon settlement archaeological finds do indicate activity of that period.

Both this place and Thetford itself fulfill the requirements of a mustering point, ease of access, central location and easily identifiable. The advantage of the mustering point being at Knettishall rather than Thetford is simply the sheer chaos caused by the introduction into a township of a large body of troops. Alfred's mustering point of 'Edgebrightstone' also appears to have been a spot in the open rather than in a major settlement. The possibility of one of these two sites being the location of the mustering point is pure conjecture but it would help to explain the Danish army settling at Thetford after their victory. According to the Anglo-Saxon Chronicle the Danes made their winter camp at Thetford. It then goes on to tell us that King Edmund fought the Danes that year and was defeated. What the Chronicle does not make clear is the order in which this happened. We know there was a battle and this is traditionally supposed to have taken place in the Thetford area but whether this was the Danes attacking Edmund's growing army and newly gathered supplies or Edmund attacking the winter quarters of the Danes is unclear.

If we look at the previous campaigns of the Danish army it does become clear that they were a large, well prepared force that probably outnumbered Edmund's Saxon militia. The **'Chronicle of Aethelwold'**, part of the Anglo-Saxon Chronicle, does state that **'Edmund the king decided war against them [the Danes]'** and this does seem to place Edmund in the role of aggressor and yet the combined force of Mercia and Wessex had been unable, or unwilling, to try and oust the Danes from defensive positions at Nottingham and the Northumbrian army had been routed trying a similar venture at York. It is therefore highly unlikely that Edmund would have tried and attack an army larger than his own while it was entrenched behind the defences at Thetford.

The **'Chronicle of Aethelwold'** could simply mean that by raising his army Edmund was preparing to fight the invaders. It does not necessarily mean that he was the first to launch an attack. Thetford was defended by rivers to the north, marshes to the south east and earthworks all around. We must conclude that, barring a major military blunder on Edmund's part, it was the Danes who attacked the encamped army of the Saxons.

If Edmund had chosen to gather his troops near the river crossing at Knettishall then his position would have been all the more precarious. Although he did have high ground on either side of the river and, due to the narrowness of the crossing point, a restricted frontage to protect he would be without major defensive works and trying to command a newly raised militia.

Edmund's force was raised mainly of levy men who two weeks earlier would have been busy at their various trades. They had not been involved in warfare of any size for over a decade and even if they were present at the siege at Nottingham two years previously there had been no fighting to speak of. When the Danes had originally landed in East Anglia they had been forced to make peace.

Taking all this into consideration it was probably a rather nervous and apprehensive army that faced the Danes on that autumn morning in 870.

The 'Great Force'

The actual number of Danes who landed in East Anglia in 866 has been the subject of much debate. Numbers have variously been suggested as high as 20,000 and as low as 500. Yet with modern archaeological finds being taken into account, combined with original source material, it is possible to calculate with a degree of accuracy the probable size of the invading force.

When battles took place and were recorded in the Anglo-Saxon Chronicles they do not usually mention the numbers that took part in the conflict but instead refer to the number of ships companies that formed the force. For example, in 836 King Eegbryht fought against 25 ships' companies. In 840 Ealdorman Wulfheard fought against 37 ships' companies and in 843 another Ealdorman of Wessex fought against 35 ships' companies.

In recent years several discoveries have been made of the remains of longships from around the period of the invasion and these finds have led to replicas being built. One of the earliest of replicas to be produced was a copy of a ship discovered in a burial mound in Norway and has become known as the 'Gokstad' ship. Clinker built of oak she was about 78 feet in length with a beam of 16 feet, and carried between 40 and 50 warriors. In 1893 she was successfully sailed, as an experiment, from Norway to the U.S.A. With the help of contemporary evidence and such modern replicas it is possible to estimate the crew numbers of the average warship.

Longships were by no means of consistent dimensions and craft capable of making the North Sea crossing have been discovered as ranging from 40 to 100 feet in length. A longship of 40 feet would be considered small by raiding standards yet could hold up to 20 men. At the other extreme a 'Dragonship' of 100 feet could easily transport 60 men across the sea. From this we may estimate that the average raiding longship would carry somewhere in the region of 50 warriors and probably be very similar to the 'Gokstad' ship. These ships were designed for rapid manoeuvrability in close coastal waters, yet could just as easily cross the Atlantic.

The actual number of longships that made up the 'Great Force' is a little more difficult to estimate with confidence. The actual numbers of ships that took part in military actions in the years before the invasion of 866 are well recorded in the Anglo-Saxon Chronicles. This is presumably because the capture of an enemy ship meant a healthy profit for the victor and such engagements would have been recorded with accuracy. Yet when, in 851, the "greatest army yet seen" landed in Kent and sacked Canterbury it is declared that they had over 350 ships. This seems unrealistic as such a force of ships would have carried more troops than the entire population of London, Norwich and Thetford combined. This number seems even more unlikely when later in the same year King Aethelstan fought and defeated a 'great force' after the capture of only nine ships. As sinkings in battle were unusual it is probable that the Danes withdrew after losing a significant number of their fleet. This would imply that "the greatest army yet seen" had closer to 50 ships rather than 350. It must then be noted that these 350 ships that were said to have landed in Kent were never actually engaged in battle.

The battle of Countisbury Hill in 878 is one of the few cases where we are given both the actual number of troops involved and the number of longships used to transport them. It is stated that the Danish army of 1200 men arrived in a fleet of 23 ships which gives an average complement of 52 men and also supports the idea that each ship carried about 50 warriors.

It has been suggested that the 'Great Army' must have been made up of a much higher number than is now generally accepted. Some historians find it hard to believe that an army of less than 2000 men can be described as a 'Great' force yet Scandinavian sources also agree with the general amount of ships used in a major campaign. In the Norse saga of 'Bosi and Herraud', written in about 1300, it is declared that the heroes have gathered a 'Huge' army which they then sail off with in 40 ships. This 'Huge' army obviously consisted of about 2000 men.[11]

With these figures of previous raids it is then possible to estimate the numbers of longships used to transport the 'Great force' of 866. They are not reported as being the 'largest army yet', a fact hardly likely to pass by the chroniclers, but are still large enough to to earn the descriptive title of 'Great'. The probable number of longships used is therefore likely to have been between 35 and 45, which, if we take an average of 50 warriors per ship, suggests a total force of between 1750 and 2250 troops.

If this number is then considered to be the basic core of the army that landed in 866 then we can add to this reinforcements from Northumbria and those who landed in the years between 866 and 869. It is likely then that the force that marched on East Anglia was in excess of 2500 men.

Although by modern standards this force may seem a little small, by contemporary standards it was larger than the average, and when compared to the probable forces available to Edmund it may be reckoned as formidable.

Edmund's army

To calculate the size of the army available to Edmund we must look at the entire Anglo-Saxon system of raising troops. Unlike many other aspects of the later Anglo-Saxon period we do have a large amount of information concerning this and we may judge with reasonable accuracy the resources Edmund could muster.

The typical Anglo-Saxon army was made up of two types of troops, the 'Hearthweru' and the 'Ceeorls'. 'Hearthweru' means literally the hearthguard, the personal household troops of the king or nobleman. The numbers of these select troops available to each king or nobleman's household varied between 50 and 200 warriors. They were the professional soldiers drawn from the upper classes and trained all their lives for warfare. These personal household troops are the direct ancestors of the 'thegns' who fought at Hastings and in turn developed into the knightly class of the later middle ages.

The 'Ceorls', on the other hand, were the militia troops raised from the lower classes of the free landholders. These 'Ceorls' made up the bulk of the later Anglo-Saxon armies and strict laws governed their call up. The first ordinance relating to the legalities of raising troops, or the 'Fyrd', appears in the 'Laws of King Ine of Wessex' written in 694.

This document legally required all men between the ages of 15 and 60 to attend for a limited period of military service. This massed levy of the whole population is known today as the 'general fyrd'. As the kingdoms developed this form of levy was realized to be too binding on the whole population. An entire kingdoms agriculture and commerce could grind to a halt for several months and so it was gradually replaced by, what we call today, the 'select fyrd'. This was a more selective call up that allowed the majority of the population to continue working and thereby support those who had been called away for military service. This led to a better provisioned and better armed force available for longer periods of service. By the late ninth century the 'general fyrd' had been all but done away with and it is likely that Edmund's army was raised using the 'select fyrd' method.

Much of what is known today of this 'select fyrd' comes later from the 'Domesday Book' entry for Berkshire written in 1089. This entry stated: **'if the king sent an army anywhere, one soldier went from five hides, each hide providing four shillings towards his wages and subsistence for two months'**.

The hide was a unit of land that traditionally was the amount needed to support a freeman and his family. Although of no fixed size it traditionally measures about between forty and one hundred and twenty acres. These five 'hides' would supply, equip and provision one soldier. When twenty of these five hide units were grouped together they became known as a 'Hundred'. Each shire was made up of a varied amount of these Hundreds and by multiplying the number of Hundreds by twenty a guide to the number of troops raised by the 'select fyrd' may be obtained.

In the Domesday Book for Norfolk 35 Hundreds are listed and although this probably represents a larger number than there were two centuries earlier it can be taken as a general guide. Some Hundreds, such as Greenhoe North and Greenhoe South, are obviously divisions of single Hundreds of an earlier period and as there are six such Hundreds in Norfolk by 1089 we may reduce the number from 35 to about 30.

If all these Hundreds sent the required number of troops Edmund would have been able to muster 600 'Ceorls' from Norfolk alone.

When combined with a similar number from Edmund's Suffolk Hundreds and his personal 'Hearthweru' this would indicate that he would have been able to muster about 1400 troops. This figure is the probable maximum number available in favourable conditions.

As we know the conditions in 870 were not favourable for the raising of an army as parts of Edmund's kingdom was already in Danish hands and no troops would be readily available in those areas. It was also the case that in the ninth century that considerable areas along the coast and in the broads were virtually uninhabited owing to Danish raids and the inhospitable countryside. It is only later that many of these areas became more than sparsely populated.

We also know that a major factor against Edmund was time. He would have had little warning of the Danish incursion into East Anglia and although he may have been in a general state of readiness the raising of troops was a lengthy business. With the Danes' rapid advance across Mercia and determined attack across the fens Edmund can have had little more than a week's warning of the approaching army.

With this in mind we may assume that Edmund's force was somewhat smaller than the maximum 1400 troops. A more realistic figure of the size of army available to him is between 1000 and 1300 troops. Although not a great force this was still a considerable size for an Anglo-Saxon army of the day. The 'Laws of King Ine' describe an army as any group of more than 35 armed men.

The Witness

I really do not know if I should go on with my tale. Perhaps some things are best forgotten about. Lost forever with the death of those men that remember them. This is perhaps one of those tales.

Yet Aelfric used to tell me that nothing is forgotten. Not completely forgotten. Ever. Always it will find a way of surviving. Tales cannot be killed as you would a man. When a man is struck down then that is the end of him. He is dead. His soul, or spirit, will pass on to wherever it is destined to go and all you are left with is a pile of flesh and bones that will soon become so much worm food. Stories are different.

No matter how many times you try to kill a story it will always somehow manage to escape. It may change in the process, bits added, characters renamed, but the story itself manages to carry on. The simple act of trying to suppress a tale or alter its content is enough to add strength to it and give it a new life. You cannot kill a story.

So it seems that the story will survive whatever I decide to do. It will be around long after I am dead and buried and so I suppose that I may as well carry on with my version of events. Far better that you hear my tale than that told by the monks that now surround me in my autumn years. The Lord knows what sort of mess they will make of it all. Have Edmund walking on water and curing the sick before I am cold in my grave no doubt.

I suppose it matters little which story survives. All are going to be tales of the same man and that can be only a good thing. He was a great and brave king and for those of us who still remember the real man that is more than enough. For those that come after he was a wise and God fearing Christian and that is also true. He was many things to many people. Perhaps that is reflected in the way that we all view him now. Warriors see him as a fighter, monks as a Christian and the Danes as a worthy opponent. He was all of those things but I do not know which he would prefer to be remembered as. Perhaps just as a caring king. A monarch who tried to do what was best for his people and although failing in so much at least setting an example for others to follow.

I ramble on so these days. Who cares what he would like to be remembered as. Its not as though he is going to get the chance to tell us. Perhaps I should have asked him at the time. Yes, I can see that going down very well. Asking your King how he would like to be remembered. A swift clout round the ear from my father and a boot up the arse from the steward is all I would have been likely to receive. So let me think on this no longer. It is not up to Edmund or myself how he or I, if at all, are remembered. That is up to those who do the remembering.

Where was I now? I lose track of myself so easily these days. One moment I set off with a purpose in one direction and by the time I get there I have forgotten why I was going there in the first place. I suppose one day I just won't get there at all and that will be that. Another old man to bury. Not that I care much anymore. At least then I will be warm.

In my youth I used to hate the heat. I never felt the cold, but now I am telling you what you already know. The heat was different. I could not stand it. I remember long summer nights that were so warm that sleep was impossible. Even lying still and naked on my palliasse would bring me out in a sweat. All energy was sapped away by the dreadful damp heat and it became impossible to get comfortable whatever I tried. The heat pressing down hard upon me, almost stifling in its intensity. Now all I feel is the cold.

It was warm the morning of the battle at Thetford. Warm and damp. It had rained slightly in the night and everything was damp about my father's hall when I arose that morning. The sky was a dull grey colour yet there was a warmth to the day that made everything damp and clammy. It was impossible to be either wet and cold or dry and warm and we suffered the worst of the two worlds. The air felt heavy and thick and it was as though the day did not really want to begin. No bright shining dawn but just a sluggish attempt at lighting the sky, duty bound and listlessly.

I was up early, there was little chance of sleep, and all about the town it appeared that everyone felt the same way. All was quiet activity, as though nothing had really stopped for the night, and although not urgent everyone seemed set upon a purpose. Everwhere the smoke from a thousand cooking fires rose up into the dull morning sky and hung there, suspended in the breezeless air, as if a great grey shroud covered the entire town. I joined the rest of our household to an early meal in the hall. Tables had been set out already and as we expected it to be a long hard day the meal was larger than was normal at that time of day.

I can remember most of the dishes that morning, apples, oat broth, pork and fresh bread, yet I do not remember eating any of them. Ale and mead were available for those of the warriors that felt they needed them but I did not take those in qauntity either. I was too nervous.

My stomach that morning was causing me some small problems. Already I had been to the yard pit three times and my guts felt in turmoil. I wanted to eat but felt that my mouth was too dry to even chew anything and my stomach too sour to hold anything down. My nerves were getting the better of me.

I had good reason to be nervous as well. We all had. This was going to be no small skirmish with a few hundred of the enemy but a full scale battle. Before, at Ely and again on the march to Thetford, I had had no choice about whether I fought or not. I had been led along by the events around me and could do nothing more than respond to whatever happened to me. This time I was going with both eyes open into a full battle. It was my choice, my decision. True, I was one of the King's armour bearers and as such would be expected to be present to serve Edmund but I was still very young. I was young even for an armour bearer and younger still to be on a battlefield. If I became suddenly ill, or found some other excuse to make myself scarce, I was sure that no one would look too long or hard in my direction. After all I had proved myself at the fight at Ely.

Perhaps it would have been better if I had disappeared that morning. It would have changed nothing at all but at least I would have been out of the worst of it.

I would not have had to witness all that I did and perhaps in some way my life would have turned out differently. As it was my pride would not let me back out of the fight.

Perhaps it is wrong to say that it was my pride that stopped me. It was really my pride in my father that kept me pressing on forward when all common sense and reason dictated for me to run and find a bolt hole. I was immensely proud of my father, what son would not be proud of such a man, and I knew that all my actions reflected upon him. I had shared in his glory and good fortune and I could do nothing now except try and live up to what was expected of his son. To avoid such a fight as we now all faced would do nothing to harm his reputation but, in turn, it would do nothing to add to it. I just wanted him to be as proud of me as I was of him.

It was that thought that led me on that morning. Not as simply thought out and clear cut as I now see it but it all boiled down to the same thing. Elinor, Aelfric and my father. They were the reasons that I carried on all that dreadful morning. They are what forced me to join the other warriors and go forth to meet with the rest of the army.

As I rode forth from the town I think my mind was a blank. No longer did the thoughts rush through my head but I was overcome with a feeling of almost serenity. I was as calm and subdued as all those about me.

I joined the army on the small hill to the south of the town and began to search through the mass of warriors for my lord theKking. Finding him was no easy matter for it seemed that the whole world was gathered on that hillside that morning. Well over a thousand warriors were present, all milling about trying to sort out their own positions, and it looked at first as though there was no order anywhere amongst them. Many were still mounted having ridden from their camps to join the gathering and this made spotting the King's party all the more difficult. I led my mount through the various groups, keeping a wary eye open for the royal banner of the three crowns, and tried to take it all in.

Warriors crowded about me, some murmering greeting, others merely staring at the pale faced youth that I must have appeared. I rode through the throng and yet did not really see it. I could not shake off the feeling of almost deathly calm and I felt as though I moved through a fog. A fog that clouded my mind as well as my sight. The only way I can now put it into words is to say that it felt much like being drunk. Not the foul mouthed, loud and overbearing kind of drunk but rather the deep slow feeling of having drunk well and retreated inside yourself. A solitary melancholic kind of drunk.

Individuals loomed out at me from the fog. Some I recognised, others that were new to me. Men I had fought beside at Ely, marched to Thetford with, shared a meal with. All swam before me amidst an overwhelming glow of steel. Steel of hauberks, steel of spearheads, steel of shield bosses. All glinted in my eyes and flashed across my dull mind. A wall of steel to face the Danes. Steel backed by the softness of flesh and blood. Steel that would eat its way into the soft flesh of the enemy.

I stumbled into the presence of the King almost without realizing it. A path had opened before me and my horse, taking the easy route, had simply followed it into the area which the King and the royal bodyguard occupied. They stood to the forward edge of the hill, overlooking the slight valley that lay to our front, and from this point Edmund intended to direct the fight.

My arrival was greeted without much enthusiasm. I was helped to dismount and a servant of my father's came forward to take charge of my horse. I recognized the fellow and expecting my father to be nearby searched the area with my eyes, seeking out his figure. My father stood just to the rear of the King. Most of the captains were present and all were close by the still figure of Edmund. Edmund stood, glorious in his finest war gear, with his eyes fixed on the distant point where the road disappeared to the south. All other eyes followed his and I soon found myself staring as hard as the rest into the distant gloom that would bring forth our enemies.

Gradually the army formed up around us. No messengers were sent, or at least I recall none, but the army fell into place along the ridge to either side of the King's position. A long thick line of shield and steel that looked, to my untrained eye, as though it could hold off the armies of all England, never mind a force of drunken Danes. I suppose that at the time I had little to compare it to but it seemed to me the greatest army ever gathered. The force that had attacked and taken Ely was nowhere near as formidable and I thought of the Danes' reaction to such a sight and felt almost sorry for them. They were going to die.

It was not just the army that inspired confidence in my young, stout heart but also our position. Edmund had chosen the site as well as he was able and I could see little to fault it. To our left ran the little river and its swampy margins, our right was covered by a steep slope and our front overlooked a shallow valley. Any attacking army would have to cross that valley and come at us directly up the slope. There was no way round for them. They would have to charge up the hill directly into the centre of our shield wall. Directly at our strongest point.

I know not how long we all stood staring into the distance but it felt like an eternity. An eternity of waiting. I had by this time taken up my own position. My position of honour. I stood just behind the King with the other two armour bearers and here we protected, or rather leant upon, the King's personal arms. My job that day was shield bearer and the King's leather covered shield now stood propped against my own spear, partly resting upon my legs.

The hours passed slowly, hushed conversations took place, men moved about amongst their fellows speculating as to what was to come. For my part I simply sank to the ground. The other lads followed my lead and soon many around us had followed suit. We all tried to make ourselves comfortable but not once did our eyes leave the southern horizon. My mind began to wander. Elinor kept appearing and disappearing in my head. Old stories told by Aelfric kept coming back to me and my mind wandered.

I found myself wandering on the shore near our manor by the sea. Hiding amongst the dunes to escape the attentions of my nurse. Sharing blackberries with my mother and dozing against the wall of the stockade. I looked back to the happy times. The times before the Danes. When the sunlight was not tinged with the blood red shade of war. A time before nightmares.

In a moment I was snapped back to the present. All around me warriors clambered to their feet. Silence descended upon the army and we all strained our eyes to the south. There, coming out of the grey mist, was a body of horsemen. Moving fast, they were bunched together, and we could make very little out. They were obviously soldiers for I could make out helmets and shields amongst them. Less than a hundred in number they descended into the little valley to our front and set their beasts to the slope before them. These were the remains of the troops sent to slow the Danes at the ford and by the looks of them they had had a hard fight of it.

They followed the road up the hill and reached the crest just to the right of where we stood. Two of the horsemen peeled off from the road and approached our royal group and we could make out what a sorry state they were all in. Few had escaped without a wound of some sort and they had ridden in such haste that their mounts were splattered with the blood of their riders. The exhausted horses' sweat mixed with the blood of the warriors and made some of the beasts look almost a shade of pink.

TheKking greeted the two warriors with great joy. At least that is what his words said but you could see there was no joy in his eyes. These two wrecks of men that now drooped before him had been part of the cream of his army. To sacrifice them in such a hopeless fight obviously hurt the King deeply. They told us that they had held as long as possible but had been pushed back as more and more of the enemy had crossed the ford. Having lost over half of their men killed and more so badly wounded that they could not fight on they had decided to retire and take their chances with the rest of the army. The Danish army was probably less than an hour behind them and if we could give them fresh shields and spears they would gladly join our ranks.

That is merely the bare bones of what they told us. The exhausted men did go into some detail concerning the fight at the ford but I heard little of it for my whole mind was taken up by the sight now before me. One of the men, the older of the two, had a great sword cut down one of his forearms. A savage blow had sliced the flesh and exposed the white of the bone from almost the elbow to the wrist. He had attempted to bind the wound but still I could see the full horror of it. As I stared a large fly settled on the bloody gash and I felt my stomach turn.

Whatever the rest of the story they told Edmund he was obviously greatly moved by it for he took a gold bangle from each of his own wrists and gave them to the warriors. The older of the two simply grasped it in his good hand unable to put it on.

The two warriors were sent to the rear of the army to find some help for their wounds and we all resumed our vigil. Our eyes scanned the southern horizon with, if possible, even more intensity. Shapes shifted, smoke drifted and before long I was beginning to see armies of heathen raiders that were not even there. I shook my head, trying to clear my vision, and my gaze returned to the south. I could make out nothing except the blurred trees and distant fields that covered the rich farmland that lay to the south of the town. Then, gradually, the mists began to take shape and out of the haze came our enemy.

They came in their hundreds. A great dark mass of them spilling forth from the hazy distance into the weak sunlight that had begun to edge its way through the sombre clouds. They advanced along the line of the road, covering a great distance to either side of the thin track. A jumble of subdued shades and shapes moving forward in a great column swamping the ground with their numbers. Their advance parties riding ahead of the mass in small groups forming the cutting edge of the wedge that was going to try and split our very bodies asunder. A dark arrowhead of violence that was aimed straight for our hearts.

More and more of the enemy came into view. The advance parties were already near the rise of the ridge opposite us, a mere half mile away, and yet still more moved out of the gloom to join their comrades. This was not the army I had seen at Ely. This made that war band look as though it had been merely one section of the whole. This was the entire might of the northern countries. All their strength together ready to take on our, now less than impressive, force. I felt my knees go weak and the muscle in my left thigh went into a spasm that I found it impossible to control. I was scared.

I had been scared before and many times since but the fear I felt that day has never again been equalled. It was almost as though I knew the outcome already. Everybody around me seemed shocked by what they were seeing. We had known that we were likely to be outnumbered but now we could see the full extent of the enemy's forces we began to realize how truly dire our situation was. We were facing almost twice the number of troops and, unlike our own army, they were battle hardened and capable.

Fear rippled through our troops like a breeze through barley. It was almost tangible. It left a dull roaring in the ears and a sourness in the pit of the stomach. We knew the challenge that we now faced and although not deterred we were subdued.

Whatever the feeling that now assailed those around him Edmund did not let it affect him. He stood stock still at the head of his army every inch the warrior King. It was from him that the army drew its strength. Just when some of the militia were ready to question the wisdom of their situation he called for his arms.

This sudden command caught all three of us unawares. We stumbled forward to arm our lord, our eyes never leaving the invaders, and helped him don his war gear and weapons. I stood by till the last, shield upraised for my lord King, and was finally released from my burden. This simple act of preparation sent a shiver throughout the entire army. Edmund was ready to face the challenge. If they stood by their King, shoulder to shoulder with their neighbours, then soon they would prevail. The King meant to fight and his men would fight for him and with him. This was a fight that had to be won. Running away would not save anyone, merely put off the inevitable. With fresh heart and glittering steel we prepared to meet the enemy.

The Danish advance seemed to take forever. They came on steadily until they reached the rise opposite ours and there they formed themselves for battle. Hundreds of men spilled along the ridge moving east and west until the whole ridge was lined with warriors and still they came. Their centre was dotted with standards and banners, a great dark raven, a horse's head, all drifting above a sea of spearheads. A great wall of shields formed ahead of us. A solid mass of colours and shapes, blacks and yellows, reds and blues. All formed into a long line that looked as though it could hold off the very tide. We stood and watched the greatest army in England take shape before our eyes.

We had no choices now. We were committed to the fight. Their horses had been taken to the rear but if we broke then they would soon be used in pursuit. A fast ride to cut down a fleeing enemy. I tried to banish such thoughts from my mind. Our time for choice was over. All we could now do was stand as stoutly as we could behind our own shield wall and wait for the attack. Wait for the onslaught.

It came soon enough but not from where we had expected it. Or at least not from where I had expected it. All of a sudden a shiver ran down the left flank of the enemy and then it was moving. A great shout rang out from a thousand Danish throats and a mass of warriors hundreds strong was charging down into the valley, trotting shoulder to shoulder, ready to hit our shields as an unstoppable mass. They came on up the gentle slope gathering speed as they neared and then, just as had happened at Ely they began to slow. Their hesitation cost them dear. Had they hit our right at the charge then I doubt that it would have stood. It was here that Edmund had placed many of the militia men, backed by professionals admittedly, but troops that had little experience. As it was they met the charge with courage and gave only a few paces under the weight of the initial impact.

The fight lasted only a short while before the Danes retired down the hill in good order leaving several score dead in front of our shields. This was their way of gauging the enemy. Feeling its strengths and weaknesses. If sacrificing a few dozen men could find the fatal flaw in our defence then they deemed it well worth the loss.

When they advanced on the left we were almost half expecting it. They did much as before but this time met stiffer resistance and had a steeper slope to climb. A few small groups tried to edge their way around the flank only to find themselves sinking up to their knees in the boggy ground where they made easy targets for our few archers. The main body fell back leaving more dead and injured upon the slope and nursing many smaller wounds.

Now we knew what to expect we grew confident and laughter and taunts were flung in the direction of the Danish army. Edmund stiffened the centre of his line with a few score archers to harry the expected Danish attack and we hoisted our shields into position to meet the onslaught. As it was it again did not happen as we had expected it. Instead of a general attack upon our centre we witnessed hundreds of figures running forward from the entire length of the enemy line. They had decided to send their archers forward to send death amongst the whole of our army.

The lightly armed bowmen only advanced as far as the first gentle rise of our side of the valley and there took their stand. Arrows were pushed into the soft earth for ease of reach and it was not long before the first deadly iron-tipped shafts came hissing into our tightly packed ranks. We could do nothing but raise our shields and hope that God was with us. It was all a game of luck. The archers merely aimed in our general direction, the slope made direct aiming difficult, and loosed their shafts. The chances were that they would hit a shield at the very least. Screams started throughout the length of our lines as arrows found softer marks and men began to fall or be helped to the rear.

I suppose that the archers did no real damage. They probably killed less than three score throughout the entire day but the effect they had upon the whole army was much larger. True, some of the wounded were too hurt to carry on but most, unless hit in the head, soon returned to the ranks. The real effect of the arrows was upon the minds of the warriors. It is one thing to stand face to face with your enemy and try to kill him but it is another matter entirely to stand still and simply let bowmen shoot in your general direction. It is the anticipation that is the worst thing. Never knowing if the next shaft is for you or not. Just standing still, shield raised high, hoping that it is someone else who is hit. It is a curious thing that I have noticed in many battles but you can never hear the arrows that are coming in your direction. They just arrive without warning. You can often hear the shafts that are landing a distance to either side of you, a sort of soft throbbing, like the distant beat of a goose wing in flight, but you never hear those that come straight for you.

Edmund seemed to be their particular target. The standard and the area around it suffered heavily from the attentions of the bowmen and it was not long before people around me began to fall. One of the other armour bearers was hit in the cheek, a slight gash that produced more tears than blood, and he was led away to the rear screaming curses at the Danish animal lovers. I was lucky throughout the whole storm of shafts. A single arrow clattered uselessly against my shield, having been deflected from another warrior's helmet, but other than that no shaft really came near me. This made me more uneasy as the minutes passed for I expected to be hit. I was standing so close to the King that it would be unthinkable to escape a minor wound. My belly was knotted tight with tension.

For some the strain became too much. Warriors who would otherwise be deemed strong and steadfast under the most arduous of onslaughts lost their heads. A few fled to the rear but most, anger boiling away their good sense, charged down the slope at the offending bowmen. A few, a very few, made it down to the bottom of the valley where they managed to revenge themselves on several of the tunic clad bowmen but most were simply shot down with a hail of true aimed shafts before they had made it halfway. They stumbled, rolled and slid to a final bloody halt on the slope to our front. Their blood rage finally cooled as the iron arrowheads spilt their lifeblood on the grass.

When the storm of arrows finally eased off and eventually ceased altogether I saw that the battle madness had spread to the Danish army as well as our own. The bowmen had withdrawn through the ranks only to be replaced by an almost holiday spectacle. Along the whole enemy front capered what I first thought to be demons. Half man and half animal. Men leapt about waving their arms, tearing off their clothes, screeching curses at the skies. Some wore nothing at all, others great bear skins while one group, who seemed to be acting as a sort of pack, were dressed in the skins of wolves. These mad men and fanatics, driven from their senses by God knows what foul enchantments launched themselves upon our lines.

Seldom have I seen such ferocity as I witnessed that day during the attack of the wild men. They simply threw themselves on our lines. Sprinting up the hill, clad only in their skins, they battered into our shield wall yelling curses at the tops of their voices. Most were cut short as they were pierced with a dozen blades but a few burst through our line to pass out savage blows with axes and swords before being overcome. One great beast of a man, clad in a greasy bear skin made straight towards the standard. An axe in either hand he threw himself bodily against our shields and managed to flatten one man, slice another in the face with a wild axe blow and hack at the standard staff before being impaled by over half a dozen spears. His screams echoed long and loud and it was the King himself who finally put an end to it by thrusting his sword down deep through the madman's eye socket. I threw up, my vomit mixing with the man's blood on the grass.

By the time I had recovered myself and managed to survey the scene everything was on the move. The Danes obviously thought we had been softened up enough, I certainly had been, and were now advancing along the whole length of the line. Ahead of them came more of their mad men, not as before but in a more restrained mood. The whole advance was restrained. The army moved towards us like a field fire, creeping slowly but steadily. No man out of place and no shouts piercing the air. On they came reaching the valley bottom as one and then starting the slow climb as they ate up the ground that separated us.

Shield grips were checked, swords loosened in scabbards, warriors moved from foot to foot, checking their balance. Then they were halfway up the slope. They began to move faster, their line becoming slightly ragged as some pressed forward eagerly. The wildmen were almost upon us and we steadied ourselves for the impact. Twenty paces behind came an entire army.

Then they hit us. In the last few strides the wild men broke into a run before hurling themselves bodily, axes whirling, into our lines. Most were cut down, a few pushed gaps into our ranks and before we could close them the Danish army was upon us. At the moment of impact a thousand voices let forth their furious war cries and we felt a shudder along the whole line as the two armies met. The holes made by the wild, dead men were now filled with struggling Danish warriors. Axes swung to widen the gaps and bloody tears began to appear in our ranks. We gave ground.

We gave ground but we made the Danes pay for every backward step. They paid with their flesh and they paid with their blood. To my left a Danish face disappeared in a welter of blood and bone as a shield boss caught him unawares. His hands tried to cover his own horror as he dropped his shield and spear only to have both removed by a well placed sword cut.

I stood in the second rank, trying to force my spear point through the Danish shields. Edmund was to my right, the centre of a struggling knot of his household troops. I saw his sword, weak sunlight reflecting on the inlaid silver, rising and falling, bloody to the hilt. A Dane literally threw himself over two of Edmund's own warriors to get at the King. One of the warriors disappeared, sliding downwards between the tightly packed shields, blood frothing from his nose and mouth. The Dane's face became a tight knot of pain. His mouth a dark hole of agony as he tried to scream. His axe flailed wildly in the King's direction, bouncing off his shield, and then the spearpoint appeared out of the Danes back, dark blood blooming like a flower's petals on the blue wool of his tunic.

We gave ground. Slowly but surely we were pushed backwards. Step by step the overwhelming numbers of the enemy pushed at us and we gave before them. We had no choice. For every warrior of ours that fell to the onslaught two Danes would suffer the same fate. But still we were being forced backwards. Their numbers were begining to tell. Where they could replace wounded or tired troops with fresh we could not. We had no reserves, no extra troops upon whom we could call for support. We had only the warriors that we had begun the battle with and gradually they were being worn down.

The centre of the fight was about the royal standard, that much was obvious for all to see, but what was going on elsewhere along the line was a mystery to me. My entire world was confined to the few dozen warriors that surrounded myself and the King. Each of those men was a proven warrior of high rank, tested in their field and expert with all kinds of weapons yet even these elite troops had begun to suffer. Strength was beginning to ebb from them and their reactions began to slow. If any of them became too slow then that would end it for them. Fresh Danish troops were being thrown against the centre every few minutes and these quick witted, watchful warriors would single out one of our men who looked past his best and charge in with such fury that more than once one of Edmund's hearthguard would fall beneath the initial flurry of blows.

What damage I myself did to the heathens I do not really know. I jabbed my spear forward over the front rank whenever I espied what I thought was a gap between the enemies' shields. More often than not I was met by the jarring thud of my spearpoint hitting the wood and leather of a shield and my arm ached with the repeated rapid movements. I know that I did at least wound some of the enemy for my spearhead was bloody to the socket but I doubt that after the first ten minutes I had the strength to do more than lightly wound them. My arm ached, my eyes were blurred with sweat and once more the fog came down around me.

The dream turned into a nightmare. Everything around me slowed down to a snail's pace. I was aware of everything. Each blow that fell, every flying droplet of blood, every scream, but all came at me across a void. A long dark tunnel was before me and at the far end I could see myself. A tall lanky, sweat stained youth, thrusting forward with his spear, eyes wide with shock, blood splattering his hands and shield. A youth where only men should tread.

I was brought back to myself with a jolt. The noise of battle had increased dramatically to our right. The troops to our front withdrew a few paces, breath rasping harshly from their throats and sweat and spittle flecking their beards.

103

Those around me took glances to our right. Trying desperately to see what was going on. The Danes to our front were also glancing in that direction. It was as though both sides had drawn back to take in the new situation, to try and understand what was going on.

We learnt the truth quickly enough as the Danes gave a triumphant cry and fell on more heavily than ever. Our right flank had collapsed.

For Edmund and all those who fought by his side, we knew at that moment that we had lost the battle. With our right wing now in tatters we realized it was only a matter of time before the Danes would add fresh troops to the fight at that end of the line and roll up our entire army. Our only option was to try and withdraw in as much order as we could muster and retire upon the town. In the best of conditions that would have been difficult but now with the Danes screaming victory in our faces and the right wing folding back on itself we knew it would be near impossible.

It started as a gradual edging backwards. As the right wing fell back in disorder the centre tried to compensate by swinging around to face the new threat but all was in vain. The militia troops had lost their heart to fight. We could only keep edging backwards fighting every step of the way. Our losses grew as we became more strung out and gaps began to appear in our ranks. The Danes pressed ever harder forward, scenting a complete victory and wanting it over with quickly. We tried to hold them. A large body of the hearth guard pressed around the King and his standard stalling all attempts by the Danes to reach his royal body. I fell back with them, a new strength, a strength borne of fear, now moving my tired limbs with a renewed vigour. I lashed out at any of the heathens that came within reach. One I caught across the face, laying open his cheek with the razor edge of my spear, and we moved ever backwards. And then it was over.

What the signal was I do not know. It just happened all of a sudden. It was like a swollen river bursting its banks. No gradual trickle but a sudden torrent that sweeps all before it. One moment we were edging our way backwards, thrusting and parrying, and the next moment the army just dissolved. No longer was it a gallant band of warriors but rather just a rushing mass of fleshy targets.

I ran with the rest. I ran with the King. The hearthguard stayed together but they were probably the only group of men that still resembled warriors. We ran over a ground littered with shields and spears, swords and axes, all cast away to make flight easier and swifter. We ran for our horses, we ran for our very lives.

What saved us that day I will never really understand. Perhaps it was the speed with which the whole line suddenly melted in front of the Danes. Perhaps we were just faster runners. Whatever the truth of the matter we did get a head start on the enemy. In the few seconds delay caused by the Danes' surprise we gained valuable yards and by the time they were in full pursuit we were a full twenty yards ahead of them.

Not all were so lucky of course. The wounded and the slow were slaughtered as they fled. Bodies hurling down into the turf as spears pierced their backs. Those that stumbled or fell lasted only seconds before their end came mercifully swiftly beneath the Danish axes.

We ran onwards, breath tearing harshly at my already straining lungs, and not daring to look back. The horses had of course gone. Taken by those who had the foresight to realise early what was happening. I had nearly tripped over the body of one of the grooms, cut down by a desperate warrior from his own side, and it was only by sheer luck that I managed to remain upright. To fall was to die. Down the slope we fled. Away from the vengeful axes of the pursuing Danes. Our feet almost leaving our tired bodies behind as we fled for the safety of the town walls.

The town was not far off now. Another hundred yards or so and we would be safe behind it's stout timber walls. Ahead of us I could make out the dark swarm of warriors funnelling through the gate. A rough heaving mass all seeking the safety of the walls. Men were trying to close the gates upon them. Panic flashed through my mind. Don't close the gates, Don't close the gates. If we were left outside we would surely die. Panic had siezed those already in the town and they wished the gates secured no matter the cost to those left outside.

One gate was closed already. The other was still wide, blocked by the struggling mass of men who tried to crowd through the opening. Blows were being exchanged, blood being spilt. The panic from those trying to enter was spreading backwards and men were clawing at each other to push their way forward. Those still armed used them to bloody effect. Screams filled the air and I tasted the salt of the desperate tears as they ran down my face. We were almost at the crowd. Soon we would join those others in the fight around the gate. Soon we too would be trying to fight our way to safety. This was a struggle that would respect no rank and no position. I tensed myself to fight as hard as the rest. I did not want to die. Not here and not now.

Suddenly I was catapulted to my right. I managed to keep my feet but only just. A strong hand had grabbed hold of my shoulder. Thinking I had finally been caught by a fleet footed Dane I tensed my body for the killing blow that I expected to follow. I tried to struggle but the fight had gone from me. Then I glanced around and instead of the triumphant Danish face I expected to see was the anxious, strained face of my father. He urged me onwards further to the right of the main body of the army. Edmund and a few surviving members of his guard were with us, the standard gone, we made our way out of the main mass of fleeing warriors and headed for the right hand side of the town walls.

We ran on, my legs no longer feeling of any thing, but still we kept onwards. We came to the river within minutes and without waiting or hesitating plunged head first into it and struck out for the far bank. I panted my way up the muddy bank and it was there that I first drew breath. Not all those that had entered the river made it to the otherside. Some either too tired or weighed down by their mail armour had perished but most of us now lay retching and panting upon the muddy grass.

We had not been pursued across the river by the enemy. A few of the Danes must have seen us make our escape but they showed little interest in us. They were far too busy slaying our comrades around the gateway. From our position we could just make out the gate. It had still not closed and now it was so full of stuggling men that it had no hope of being shut. As the Danes waded into the slaughter I knew that the town was lost. They would soon take the open gate, there was no one there who could stop them, and then the town would fall to their passions and their slaughter. As I watched I saw the first of the heathens pushing and slashing their way through the open gateway, yells of brutal victory issuing from their throats and I knew that Thetford was lost.

Lying panting and exhausted upon the muddy bank I wept. I wept for the town and I wept for the sheer stupidity of it all. Everything was lost. What before had seemed so sensible and so glorious now just looked so stupid. The vain thoughts of an untried youth.

Old as I am now I can look back and see that that was the moment that I did my last bit of growing up. I had fought and done my best, we all had, but still we had lost. Life was not the true romance of Aelfric's tales but a bloody combat of survival. Life was not fair. What more could we have done? At the time I knew that what I was watching happen before my very eyes was a dread sight. A town being laid waste and put to the sword. Now I am older I know the dreadful truth of what was really happening behind those walls. In my youth my imagination could not match the true horror of it. I have seen towns taken since, even taken some myself, and my only wish that I send back through the years is that I hope for those that I knew and loved that the end came quickly. I hope it was quick for Elinor.

Years afterwards I started to ask questions of those that survived the sack of Thetford about the events that happened inside the walls. The tales were all desperate and truly sad but they told me little. I even took to questioning some of the Danish warriors I met about their victory but by the time a peace was signed several years later the edge of their memories had been blunted by many more such victories.

I did meet with one Dane who remembered the fight well enough though. He had been hamstrung in the fighting in the town and so it had been his last battle and remained clear in his memory. He said he thought he remembered passing my father's hall. My description of it touched his memory, for it was a well set up place, but all he could say was that the yard was full of bodies and smoke had been billowing from the doorway. After hearing his tale I questioned people no further. If Elinor died in the attack, and I am almost sure she did, I hope she did not suffer. I hope it was quick and as painless as possible.

As we dragged our tired bodies further up the bank of the river and into the cover of some scrub bushes I thought no such thoughts. I merely wanted to kill more Danes. To escape this foul place and come back with an army. To follow my King and revenge this defeat. The tears still ran down my dirty cheeks but now they were filled with as much rage and hatred as they had once been filled with self pity.

The Battle

Nothing is really known of the actual battle between Edmund and the Danish army except that it was fought 'Atrociter' [all out] and that it resulted in defeat for the East Anglians, however from contemporary evidence it is possible to piece together what a battle of the period might have been like. Edmund was outnumbered and facing a more confident, better trained force that would immediately place him at a disadvantage and on the defensive.

Whichever side was on the defensive would have tried to choose and defend the higher ground with the intention of wearing down the attacking troops by requiring them to charge uphill. This was common practice at a time when both sides fought on foot and would have been one of the few natural advantages available.

We know much of each sides' military tactics from various poems and sagas, such as **'the battle of Maldon'** [12], that have survived to the present day. Combining this with the archeaological evidence we find that the majority of troops would have fought on foot with spear and shield. The shield and spear are by far the commonest types of weapon discovered in Anglo-Saxon graves. The shield was of wood, often lime, and had a pointed central iron boss that served as both an offensive and defensive weapon. The shield was often covered in leather and decorated with simple colours and patterns. The spear was usually of ash, or a similar tough wood, and was about six feet in length with a iron head and often an iron ferrule at the base. It was the wooden shields and spear shafts that took the majority of the battle damage and after a major encounter many would need repair or replacement.

Only those of higher rank or social class tended to use swords or axes. The sword was a costly piece of equipment and not to be afforded by all. They were so precious that they tended to be handed from one generation to the next. A sword belonging to King Offa of Mercia was later bequeathed in the eleventh century from a prince to his brother, and swords of age were considered to have virtues of their own. Some swords had such a character in their own right that they were given names as in the case of the two swords used by Beowulf, 'Hrunting' and 'Naegling'.

These swords were often decorated and encrusted with precious metals and engraved with patterns and mottoes. Carried on a decorated belt or sling they were housed in scabbards made of wood and then covered with leather.

In some cases the richer Anglo-Saxons were buried with their swords and it is from these burials that we can really gauge how rare swords were. Of the 308 graves excavated at Kingston only two contained swords and in the 150 graves excavated at Bifrons they discovered only seven burials containing swords.

As with swords, other items of protection such as helmets and mail armour, were reserved for the select few who could afford them. Much more common were bows and javelins and although the bows were less favoured by the Saxons they are likely to have been used by the lower classes. Danish use of the bow has been well recorded in many battles and it appears to have been used by all classes of warrior without distinction.

The Saxon troops probably drew up their lines in what was called the 'Scildburh' [lit. shield-fort] which was a series of dense blocks of troops. These blocks were usually made up of men from the same locality who stood so close that their shields almost overlapped. This combining of soldiers from the same locality was intended to strengthen the morale as they would be fighting next to their relations and neighbours. The front ranks of these 'Scildburh' contained the best armoured troops and is possibly where the professional household troops were located, although it is often recorded that they formed a separate unit and fought in the most exposed of positions as an example to the rest of the army.

In the poem **'The battle of Maldon'**, written in the tenth century, the Saxon commander Byrhtnoth is said to have **'alighted where he loved best, and was held most at heart - among his hearth companions'.**

The Danish tactics were very similar to the Saxon but instead of the separate blocks they seem to have favoured a single line made up of a series of wedges. The commanders would position themselves at the front apexes of the wedges as an example to their men. This wedge formation was also, at times, used by the Saxon troops but usually when they had a larger proportion of trained, battle hardened men within their force. The 'Scildburh' formation relied less upon the individual and was therefore better suited to Edmund's army.

Once both sides were drawn up there seems to have been little manoeuvring for position. In the 'Battle of Maldon' poem the Saxon commander, Byrhtnoth's, main piece of advice to his men was as to how they should hold their shields and stand firm and had little to do with tactics.

**'Then Byrhtnoth dresses his warrior band
from horseback taught each man his task
where he should stand, how keep his station
He bade them keep their linden-boards aright
fast in finger-grip, and not in fear'.**

The accepted next move was for one side or other to advance upon the enemy. As the two forces neared each other projectiles would be thrown and javelins hurled at the foremost ranks of the enemy with the hope of creating a gap in the shield wall. Then the two sides would close with a crash as the shield walls met and hand to hand fighting would begin in earnest.

Again from the 'Battle of Maldon'-
**'They let the file hardened spears, the grim ground javelins,
fly from the hand. Bows were busy, point pierced shield,
The rush of battle was fierce, warriors fell on all sides.
The young men lay dead'.**

Fighting of this sort was a bloody affair and the wounds inflicted could be horrendous.

In July 1361 another force of Danish invaders fought and defeated an army at Wisby on the Swedish island of Gotland. Due to the hot summer weather the dead were hastily thrown into grave pits without being stripped of their armour. Recent excavations of the remains of over 1800 of the skeletons has given us a unique view of the injuries sustained in hand to hand combat.

Much research was carried out on the remains by archaeologist Bo Ingelmark and from the findings of this research it is possible to reconstruct some of the causes of death. Many of the remains show multiple wounds that have cut deep enough to scar the bone and many of the head wounds appear to have been delivered when the victim was prostrate. In four cases the nose had been severed by a single blow, and one tremendous blow, possibly from an axe, had severed both the victim's legs just below the knees. The evidence for archery is slim and most of the skeletons that do show hits from projectiles tend to be wounded in the skull area. This is probably due to the fact that arrow wounds upon the fleshy parts of the torso would not show up on the skeletons. Such research gives us a vivid impression of the type of bloody conflict as fought by Edmund and the East Anglian army.

As the battle drew on the greater experience and numbers of the Danes began to make their mark. Edmund's troops started to be pushed back leaving their dead where they lay. The 'scildburhs' were being pushed into ever smaller knots of struggling men and the ground had become slippery for the leather-soled boots as they tried to find grip on the blood soaked grass. Gradually the edging backwards became a fully fledged retreat as Edmund's army broke before the Danes. For the Saxons the battle was over and the corpse-strewn field was left to the Danish victors.

As with other battles of the period it is likely that the dead were left where they fell. The Danes would bury their comrades with their full pagan rites and be assured of their spirits passing into the next world but the Saxon dead were shown no such consideration. After the battle at Hastings in 1066 the victorious Normans allowed the locals to remove their dead for burial but those not so claimed were left on the field to rot. Writing seventy years afterwards Orderic Vitalis [13] told of piles of bleached bones that were still to be seen.

This disrespect for the enemy dead served several purposes. It acted as a visual reminder to the population of the cost of opposing the invaders and the results they could expect if they did the same. It was also a calculated insult, as both Pagan and Christian Saxons believed that without proper burial rites the spirits of the slaughtered would remain forever earthbound. To deny the defeated a proper burial was a sign of the victor's power over the Saxons even after death.

All the accounts of the death of Edmund claim that he was killed after the battle. Only the Anglo-Saxon Chronicle fails to mention whether he died during or after the fight. According to Abbo's account Edmund is left after the battle accompanied only by Bishop Humbert [14], a few priests and several of his hearth guard. A Danish messenger is said to have arrived at Edmunds camp unexpectedly and demanded that Edmund became a vassal king to the Danes. Upon Edmund's refusal the site was surrounded and Edmund captured and martyred. As Abbo's account is as near that of an eyewitness as is possible we must assume that Edmund escaped the slaughter on the battlefield and was captured some distance away as he fled for safety.

For a king to leave the field when events turned against him was not unusual. The following year King Alfred of Wessex fought against the same force many times and in most cases retired from the field. What was more unusual was for a king to fight to the bitter end when he knew all was lost.

Edmund would have retired with his personal bodyguard and left his levies to retreat in whatever order they could manage. Pursuit by the victors was an accepted part of warfare of the period and many of the fleeing troops would have been lucky to survive. It is probable that it was during this pursuit that Edmund was captured by the invaders.

The Witness.

We remained hidden in the bushes by the riverbank only long enough for us to regain what we could of our breath. All of us were exhausted by the battle and our subsequent flight and several of the warriors showed wounds upon their bodies. I too had received a wound. At some point I had been cut across the back of the hand. The wound was not deep and I had not even noticed it until I had got my breath back and felt it begin to throb. What I found most bemusing was the fact that, for the life of me, I could not remember how it happened.

This has happened to me several times in my life. I have fought in battle after battle, skirmish after bloody skirmish and been wounded more times than I can count. My body now is a mere network of scars that show up pale against my dark skin but I could not tell you how I came by over half of them. I used to almost have to sit down after a fight and check each of my limbs for damage for I felt little or no pain at the time. It is a curious effect of the fear that takes you in a battle that such things are blocked out by your mind. I felt more pain when I lost the tip of my little finger cutting bread than when I had a spear in my thigh. Until afterwards that is.

The cut across my hand did not worry me and I managed to bind it well enough before we had to move on.

There were over twenty of us hidden in the bushes by the river and our attempts at moving off quietly, without attracting the attention of the enemy, left a little to be desired. As we skulked off into the deeper cover of the woodland I glanced back in the direction of the town. By this time the fight was all but over and I noticed the first plumes of pale smoke begin to rise from behind the stockade. At least from this distance we were too far away to hear the screams. What did immediately catch my attention was a group of enemy warriors who were staring and gesturing in our direction. As I watched, one of the warriors mounted his horse and cantered off in the direction of the town. He was surely going to warn his commanders that some of us were escaping. The fact that many of us were wearing mail armour would not have escaped notice and singled us out as men of rank. As I turned my attention away from the town and concentrated upon keeping up with the rest I knew that the hunt was on.

We skirted the edge of the woodland, staying as well concealed as we could, and headed to the east. To our north was the marshland and one of the rivers, just out of sight, and to the south lay the other river. We had no choice but to head to the east, to the river crossing where we could join the old straight road and safely cross either of the rivers. The enemy could not catch us before we came to the river crossing unless they too wished to swim after us so we at least had time to catch our breath and prepare.

The river crossing was still some two or three miles off when we came across a farmstead. A large stockaded yard containing several outbuildings and a small thatched hall showed through the trees to our right. Our need for refreshment and the possibility that we might find horses there far outweighed the possible risk of approaching the farm. After all until less than an hour beforehand all this countryside had been part of Edmund's kingdom. Quite where we stood now we would find out over the next few days.

Even though we felt sure that the farmstead would be no threat to us we still took the precaution of approaching warily from the slightly higher ground to the north so that we could see any threats before they could see us. As we cleared the trees, I was one of the last, we all realized that the farm offered more than we could ever have wished for. It had obviously been used as accommodation for some of our troops in the weeks leading up to the battle and the dark patches of the now cold campfires showed black against the soft green of the turf. From the number of fires the force stationed here must have been of a considerable size and we could only hope that some of them had decided to leave their mounts behind in the previous few days' gathering of the army.

As we approached the gateway we were challenged by a spearman concealed behind the drawn back gate. He had obviously been caught unawares for his bearded face had a startled look to it and he had not even attempted to close the gates and secure the yard. This sight of a suprised and obviously fearful old warrior gave some amusement to my companions who laughed and swore at the guard and yelled insults in his direction. Hearing his own tongue and realizing how foolish he must have seemed, one lone spearmen challenging twenty, he gave us a sheepish grin and asked us what we were after.

When all had been explained to the gatekeeper we had the dubious pleasure of watching the features of his face pass through a rapid series of changes. Shock at finding himself in the presence of a king, horror at hearing of the loss of the battle and town and finally a sort of dull bewilderment as he took in the importance of the news. My father questioned him closely about the supplies and livestock to be found in the farm and within minutes some of the men were rounding up over a dozen horses. The rest of us searched the farmbuildings and hall for anything that might be of use. We found food enough for all with several day's supplies of bread and cheese, the only items that we could carry easily, and we each ate our fill on the spot. There were few arms about the place for most had been taken by the warriors when called to the army but we did find two old spears and a couple of small saxes. These were given to those who had cast away everything in the battle and now over half of us were at least armed in the most rudimentary of fashions. I still had my large sax tucked into my belt for I had only been using shield and spear during the battle and it was not until it was pointed out to me that I realised it was still there.

Within half an hour we were ready to move again. It was unsafe to stay any longer for had we been caught at the farmstead then, even though slightly defensible, it would have offered little protection and hampered our escape. The gatekeeper decided that it was safest to stay at the farm. That of course is not how he worded it but it is what he meant. He claimed that he wished to wait and see if any of his comrades would return from the fight but I could see the fear in his eyes and knew he was lying. He was right really. What chance would he have stood if captured with the defeated and fleeing king. Far safer to cast away his arms and run back home claiming to never have been near the fight at Thetford. As we rode and jogged away from the farm, setting out east once more, I rather envied him the simplicity of his decision.

Things were not so easy for the rest of us. True I would have followed wherever my father and the King led but the others had only their sense of honour to bind them to the King. Most were members of the hearthguard and so had been members of Edmund's household throughout all the good years and now that events had turned against them would never dream of leaving him to his fate. Many of them would gladly have given their lives for Edmund without question. In fact many of their long time hearth companions had done just that. They now lay on the bloody field outside the walls of Thetford.

The few others of our party who were not of the Kings personal bodyguard had no such deep seated loyalties to drive them onwards. They could have left our party at any time, pleading worries for their families or other concerns, but to give them their due, after leaving the warrior at the farm they did not even look wistfully over their shoulders.

With the addition of the horses we were moving with more speed than before. We could not travel as fast as we would have liked but by having those on foot grab a hold of each of the horses' stirrups as they jogged alongside we were able to cover much more ground than before. It was still several hours before sunset when we struck the course of the old road and it was here that we stopped once more.

We now had to decide which way we would go. I had heard my father and several of the hearthguard discussing which would be the best course of action with the King on the ride from the farm, but our halting at the road obviously meant that the King had not, as yet, made his decision.

The choice, as far as I understood it, was a simple one. We could either head to the north or the south. Neither choice was ideal but then again we were not exactly in a position to be fussy. The Danes must have begun to realize by this time that they had failed to kill or capture the King and would be in pursuit as soon as may be. To head to the south was to take us back nearer the direction of the Danish advance but it did have the advantage of taking us into the lands controlled by Wessex. In Wessex we could at least expect a reasonably warm welcome if not troops to help in our fight.

To head north did have the advantage of taking us directly away from the enemy army but little else was in its favour. To the north lay no reinforcements, no new army and the possibility of being trapped against the coast by the advancing Danes.

The decision, now I look at it through my old eyes, seems simple but at the time nothing was that clear cut. We had slept little in the last few days, fought a battle and swum a river. We were in no state to make quick or clear headed decisions. If I had to make the choice again today doubtless I would opt for travelling north, against all sense, but perhaps that is because I know what the consequences of Edmund's choice was to be. There is of course no telling what would have happened had we taken the northern route. Perhaps the outcome would have turned out much the same, perhaps not. Idle speculation for an old man to ponder on in the dark sleepless nights that now assail me so often. It is too late to change a decision made all those years ago and fruitless to think upon it. As it was Edmund decided that we should head to the south.

This decision was agreed upon by all those present as being a wise choice. On the road we could surely outrun any pursuit and be in safety in two or three days at most. Another factor that helped to influence Edmunds choice was the sight to the north of a small band of horsemen. They were still too far away to make out whether they were Danes or Saxons but their very presence was disquieting. If they were Danes then the pursuit was on in earnest and if they were Saxon then they were likely to be of little help having probably gone through much the same as us that day. Caution prevailed and we headed south to the river crossing without even waiting to discover the identity of the other horsemen.

We reached the river crossing without further incident at with at least an hour of daylight left in the sky. At the far side of the crossing, which we forded easily, it coming no higher than the foot soldiers' thighs, was a small settlement. Too mean to be described as a village if offered us the chance to call a halt for a few minutes while we scouted the area for extra mounts. We did find a few but none were of good quality and our own beasts, already tired, looked better than those did fresh. They did at least give a chance for those who had been jogging alongside to ride for a while. Edmund now decided that it would be better if the whole of his party went mounted. This would of course speed us up but would mean a reduction in the numbers of warriors available to defend the King in the event of trouble. Those who were to be dismissed argued bitterly with the King that they would run a hundred miles rather than leave his side but Edmund would have none of it.

And so when we left the settlement by the ford we were all mounted and about half a dozen fewer in number. Truth be told Edmund could see that those that had not been mounted were not only slowing our pace but also running themselves into the ground. Even by changing places with the riders every mile or so we all fared little better. Everybody was exhausted and to have allowed them to remain with us on foot was not good for all concerned. Had we come across any trouble I doubt if any of us could have put up much of a fight. So we left them by the river, all swearing their oaths of loyalty to the King and cursing the Danes, and carried on south down the road.

The road was one of the best in the kingdom, wide and dry with firm footing for our beasts and we made good progress. By the time it was fully dark we must have covered some five or so miles since we had crossed the river. We had been pushing our mounts hard and they had all sweated to a lather in the chill evening air. When it became too dark to carry on in safety we stopped at a farmstead just off the road. Both we and the horses were too tired to continue through the night at even a walk and so it was deemed best to try and sleep for a few hours and move off again as soon as the sky showed light enough. We had seen no signs of the enemy since we had crossed the river and all of us suspected that they were still busy picking over the bones of Thetford.

We attended to the horses with as much speed as possible and forced down a hasty meal before we joined the farmer and his family in the small hall for the night. Cramped and stuffy though it was I was asleep almost as soon as I lay down. So tired had I discovered myself to be upon dismounting that my legs had almost given way beneath me and it was sheer willpower that had kept me awake long enough to gulp down some of the farm's rather sour ale and eat some of the dry bread and cheese we had found earlier in the day. I slept in all my gear, with my head upon my saddlecloth and I doubt if an entire Danish army could have woken me.

I was woken before dawn by my father. He had been awake some time for he had had time to have some food and was now offering me the same. The farmer and his family had kept watch the night through so that all of us could sleep and had spent the time preparing a meal for us all. He said there was a river nearby where he caught eels and so we were treated, if that is the term, to a stew of eels and barley with fresh bread and ale. The ale had not improved during the night but we were all grateful for his kindness even if eels did remind me of our last escape from the Danes at Ely. The whole family were trying to do all they could to help us and had even found a few fresh horses for us in the night. Mind you it cannot have been everyday that the farmer had a King, even one without a kingdom, and his men staying in his hall and I doubt if he would have slept a wink anyway.

Edmund, ever the gracious lord, presented the farmer with a silver arm ring as a token of his kindness and told him that his charity would never be forgotten. Well it would not be forgotten by me, that is certain, for Edmund, having given away all his gold during the battle and at the last farm, borrowed the arm ring from me. We left the farm at dawn with blessings being shouted after us and me scowling over my shoulder.

We crossed the farmer's little river, where he caught the eels, about a mile further on and saw no one, not even a farmer. News must have been already spreading about the Danes and people deemed it wiser to stay hidden until they knew more of what was going on. From the river we pushed on south down the road.

The day was a foul one. Dull, overcast and damp. All the colour seemed to have drained out of both sky and land and there was a fine drizzly mist in the air which clung to cloaks and gave a sheen to even the roughest of the horses' coats. We did not push the beasts that morning for we knew we had far to travel and there seemed to be no immediate threat. We travelled at little more than a walking pace for the damp had made some of the stones of the road slippery and treacherous. We could not afford to lose any of our mounts in an easily avoidable accident.

Our mood became settled to match that of the land we travelled through. Normally one of the greenest and lushest parts of the east country, that day the weather and season had combined to give it an air of gloom and hopelessness. We were all still tired, even after our sleep, and for many still had to come to terms with the losses we had suffered the previous day. Some had lost family, brothers, uncles and sons, and all of us had lost many good freinds.

I was still finding it hard to believe what had taken place. Only the previous day we had all risen to meet the dawn with hope in our hearts. We were going to follow our lord King in a great victory over the Danish invaders and once and for all end the threat that hung over our splendid land. Now, a mere day later, we had lost everything we had ever held dear. We were a band of hunted men whose only chance lay in fleeing the kingdom we all loved so well. I tried to block out of my mind images of those we had lost. Aelfric, Elinor. I had no idea what had become of either of them. I tried to convince myself that old Aelfric would have had the sense to lead the others to safety when he saw the way things were going with the battle but it was of little use. My heart pleaded that they must have escaped to some safe place but my head kept telling me that the only safe place had seemed to be the town itself. Strongly defended behind earthworks and stockade and with an army between itself and the enemy it would have been the only obvious choice as a refuge. The town had fallen so quickly I doubted more than a handful had escaped.

My own mood was matched by the rest of our little company that morning. There was little talk among any of the party and the King seemed the most sombre and taciturn of us all. He was riding a little ahead of the party, eyes forward, and spoke hardly a word to any of us all morning. My father had urged his horse up beside the King's in an effort to make conversation but he had got little response for his trouble and when the King had turned to answer his questions with short blunt answers I saw that his eyes had a distant, far away look. Edmund had withdrawn himself from all of us. Wrapped in his own personal grief and sorrow.

Which of us could blame him. True, we had all lost people we cared about but he had lost everything. He had lost all his people, save the handful now at his back, and his entire kingdom. I think myself that Edmund somehow held himself to blame for what had happened. We had only ourselves to feel responsible for but he held the weight of an entire kingdom on his shoulders. Could he have done better? Could he have saved the crown? I doubt it. But that is merely my opinion. I am sure there are those who will say he could have done this or that and beaten the Danes but they were not there at the time. Those of us that were know that the King did his very best and was willing to carry on trying. Not many people can say as much as that about any soul living or dead.

We first spotted the horsemen following behind us at about midday. We had just crested a rise on one of the gentle hills that so marked out this area of the country from my north shore home when one of the warriors trailing to the rear yelled out an alarm. We all drew to a halt and followed his gaze north back along the road we had come. We could just make out a large body of horsemen a mile or so behind us. It was too far away to see any details but the fact that when they saw us they quickened their pace implied that they were not friendly. Had they been fugitives like ourselves they would most likely have avoided contact with other horsemen but these people seemed intent on catching up with us.

Edmund immediately became animated again. The following group numbered well over fifty men and in all likelyhood they were going to be better mounted than ourselves, it would be hard to be worse mounted, and so our chance of just outrunning them was remote. Even at this time of year, when the days were growing rapidly shorter, there was still a good five hours till sunset. Our only chance was to slow them down and perhaps stall their progress.

Edmund immediately ordered ten of his remaining followers to split into two groups and head off in different directions away from the road. He hoped that by splitting up the Danes would be unsure of which party to follow and perhaps if they did not choose the wrong group, then at least split their forces to search for the others. He knew he was asking much of his followers, for he wanted them to only ride away so far and then act as a bait for the pursuers. They were to keep themselves just in view of the enemy and lead as many of them as possible back to the north and east.

It was a dangerous game of cat and mouse and I did not envy those that volunteered for the task. They were tired themselves and riding sad tired horses. If they were caught they could expect little mercy to be shown them but they all seemed to be positively relishing the prospect. They cantered off to the sides of the road with grins on their faces and a flurry of cheery farewells as we gave the horses a good kick or two and broke into an unsteady canter down the road.

Our ruse obviously had some effect for when we crested the next rise or two we could make out no pursuit. They must have been drawn off by the decoys and that gave us a good extra mile or two. We managed to gain a few new mounts at a village we passed an hour or so later and this gave us all fresh heart.

The village itself had been nothing to cheer any man's soul for it was almost deserted and we had panicked the few remaining inhabitants into flight with our tales of the battle and Danish pursuit. The horses we aquired though were of good quality and it meant we could leave the worst of our nags in exchange. We grabbed a hasty meal in the saddle and set off at a good pace hoping to be off the road and in shelter by the time it got dark. We had managed to barter for some ale, meat, cheese and hard griddle cakes with the last of the inhabitants and looked forward to a more substantial meal that night.

The last few hours of our ride that day were spent looking over our shoulders and trying to keep dry. The rain had decided to make a real effort and rather than the damp invasive drizzle of the morning we were now subjected to a series of sharp little showers. This reduced the visibility further and if we were still being pursued we could not tell for we could see nothing plainly over half a mile away. I remember those last few hours very well for I had never been in the saddle almost continually for two days before and my arse hurt like hell. Whichever way I twisted and turned I could not get comfortable and even using the folds of my cloak as padding helped but little. By using my cloak as a cushion it meant that I was subjected to the full force of the rain and soon I was wet as well as uncomfortable.

Just as the light began to drain from the already dark grey sky Edmund led us off the road and set out across the countryside to the east. I knew that he had another royal manor nearby for, though I had never visited it, I had heard people talk of it as the prettiest of all his holdings. I imagined that that was where we were heading to and looked forward to a night spent in a dry warm hall. I cared not at all whether there were any beds and would have slept anywhere that was dry and did not have a saddle.

So it was that I was both disappointed and relieved when, after passing through a small wood about a mile from the road, we stopped at a small farm. Edmund had decided that it would be unwise to stay at the manor for if the Danes were pursuing him, as he was sure they were, then they too could have easily discovered the whereabouts of his royal manor. He did not wish to fall into their hands just for the sake of a dry bed and so had led us to one of its outlying farmsteads. The farm was no manor but it suited our purpose very well. It had obviously been in use until recently and, although deserted when we arrived, still held hay for the horses, enough oats to feed a small army and firewood a plenty.

We corralled the beasts in what had obviously been the cattle byre and set about making ourselves comfortable. My first need was to get dry and warm and so I took it upon myself to get the fire going. There were plenty of good dry logs stacked neatly under the overhanging eaves of the small hall and the recent occupiers had taken the precaution of laying in some dry kindling against the coming damp of the winter. I soon had a good blaze going in the small central hearth and was happily raking out cinders to heat the stones and warm the griddle cakes.

I was soon joined by most of the rest of the men who had finished settling the horses and exploring the farm and it became cramped within the hall. There was no way we could all sleep inside for the night and so some of us would have to bed down in the outbuildings. I volunteered to be one of those who slept outside for, although I would lack the warmth of the fire, I did not relish the thought of sleeping in the same small space as a dozen sweaty and damp warriors. I was assured by my grinning father that the outbuildings were all dry enough and that none of the other animals were likely to snore.

Even Edmund managed a weak smile at this rather poor jest for I had often been known to complain about my small hut at Thetford. One of the other armour bearers had had a broken nose as a child and it had never been set properly and so as a result he snored loudly enough to wake the saints. There were nights when his snores had been loud enough to wake me from deep sleep and my complaints had become a small joke about the manor. The other armour bearer slept so soundly that he would have slept through judgement day itself and I often felt bitter towards both of them.

These uncharitable thoughts about the two lads caused me to suddenly feel guilty. I had never really liked either of them, for they were several years my senior, but I had never wished any harm to come to them. As it was now they were both probably lying dead and cold on the hill outside Thetford and we sat safe and warm and made jokes at their expense. I think this sobering thought passed through several of those gathered by the fire for the meal that followed was a quiet affair even though we did discover a small barrel of mead hidden in the rafters.

Edmund returned to his silent withdrawn mood during the meal and I once again noticed how his eyes seemed to be staring at something that no one else could see. He was lost within himself and hardly managed to pull himself around when my father began to discuss plans for the next day with him. The plan was simple enough and all around the fire had a good idea what it was to be, but I think my father was using it as an excuse to draw Edmund back from wherever he had taken himself off to. I could see that Edmund's mood worried my father, for he was ever a level headed man, and this withdrawal by the King was affecting him badly. He tried to bring some animation back to the King but it seemed to have little effect.

As I said the plan was simple one and did something to raise all our spirits. We would set out at dawn at the latest and head south to the river crossing on the Stour. We would keep off the road for, although faster, it would be unsafe now we knew we were being hunted. We had no idea how far behind our pursuers were and so decided upon the slower but safer route. Once across the stour we would be in lands under the control of Wessex and could expect to find at least some troops guarding the ford. The Danes would not risk crossing into Wessex without an army at their backs and they had lost many men in the battle of Thetford. In wessex we would be safe until at least the next spring.

I think that even talk of the Stour river crossing did nothing to improve Edmund's mood for it had been close by that he had been crowned all those years before. To leave his kingdom as a fugitive within sight of the place he had sworn to be its defender must have weighed heavily upon him. We all knew that he would not desert us, that he would come back at the head of a new army to reclaim his land, but the humiliation of his present position must have been a bitter blow to his pride. He knew that the King of Wessex would welcome him with open arms, give him his support and that must have hurt his pride as much as rejection would have hurt his cause.

After the meal had been cleared away and I had set a cauldron of oats and water over the fire, so as to be ready in the morning, we all took ourselves off to sleep as best we could. This was not going to be a problem for me for I was warm, dry and well fed and felt I could sleep for a whole month. My arse was still sore from the ride but I discovered a large pile of hay in an outhouse and it allowed me to settle down comfortably wrapped in my cloak. Within minutes I was asleep.

What woke me I cannot really tell for it was still full dark and strain my ears as I could I could hear nothing. The whole farm seemed to be shrouded in silence and nothing stirred save for the occasional soft murmur as one of the horses shifted in its sleep. The rain had stopped and through the open doorway of the outhouse I could see that the sky had cleared and stars now shone brightly in the dark sky. I lay in the pile of hay staring out at the darkened yard and glittering sky when a darker shadow seemed to detach itself from the stockade's shadow and move silently across the yard towards the hall. Thinking it was but one of the warriors gone to relieve himself I lay back and tried to let sleep claim me once again. It was only as the shadow passed directly in front of the star-lit stable wall opposite my door that I could make out the shape with any clarity. Whoever the figure was he carried a shield.

My heart leapt and I felt the sudden knot of fear in my stomach. Either the Danes had caught up with us or else it was the farmers family returned in the night. Either way we were in danger. If it was but the return of the farms rightful owners then I doubted that they would mind sharing their holding with the king but at night, when both sides could mistake the other for enemies, there was no knowing what could happen. If it was the Danes then it did not bear thinking about.

I shifted my weight onto my side and attempted to try and move down the pile of hay with as much stealth as my blanket-shrouded form would allow. I managed to roll onto the floor and disentangle myself from my cloak without making too much noise and when I crawled to the door I knew I had not been observed. From my new position I could just about make out the entire stockaded yard.

The shadow had by now disappeared behind the corner of the hall and I readied myself to make a rush across the muddy yard to the hall doorway. The door was ajar for it showed as a slightly lighter strip in the end wall of the hall where the now dull glow from the fire escaped into the night. Just as I was about to move I espied another shadow moving towards the hall. I froze.

This figure also showed as carrying a shield and I could even make out the hooked shape of a Danish war axe over one shoulder. Close on the heels of this figure followed two others all similarly equipped. I shrank back into the dark shadows and my mind raced as my stomach flipped somersaults.

What was I to do? I know now that I should have shouted at the top of my lungs and tried to warn those within the hall of the danger but in such a position I also knew that by doing so I would have shortened my life considerably. I chose to stay silent. Whether from fear or simple ignorance I cannot really say but I held my tongue. Had I shouted then perhaps the King would have had a chance. Who knows. We were surrounded by a large force of Danes, or so I soon discovered, and I think it unlikely that Edmund would have stood any chance at all. As it was my options were soon to become even more limited than they had been up till then.

As I watched the shadowy figures gather together outside the doorway of the hall I was grabbed from behind. A great dirty hand was clamped over my mouth just as I was about to yell and my head was yanked sharply backwards sending a lance of pain down my spine. The Dane must have sneaked through the other door that led to the cattle byre and in my absorption with the figures outside I had been caught completely by suprise. The Dane used his free hand to clamp my arms behind my back and tears ran down my face with the pain he was causing in my shoulders.

In my agony, and through the tears, I watched as a dozen or more of the warriors in the yard kicked the door of the hall open and ran screaming into the dully lit rectangle of light.

The fight, if fight it can be called, was over in a matter of seconds. All within the hall were wrapped within their cloaks and horse blankets fast asleep. By the time they were awake and reaching for what few weapons they had they found swords and axes poised at their throats. All were captured without exchanging a blow. In the whole attack only four men died. One was the guard we had set by the gate who died in his sleep with a knife in the ribs. The other three died just as the Danes brought forth their captives from the hall. By now the yard was filling up with armed men, some bearing torches, and I was pushed out into the yard with my hands tied behind my back. As it was I did not even see the fight for it happened on the other side of the yard and my view was blocked by the rest of the captives. The Danes in their haste to capture those in the hall had not bothered to check all the outhouses thoroughly. From one of these rushed one of Edmund's hearthguard, an older man whose name I have forgotten if ever I knew it in the first place. He cut down two of the Danes before they realized what was happening and his high pitched battle cry shattered the night. He made it no further than a few steps towards the King before he too was felled by a flurry of Danish axe strokes.

Why he did it I do not know. The Danes seemed more intent on taking prisoners than killing us so he would have been safe to remain within the outhouse until discovered. Instead he chose to make his stand there, in that muddy farmyard, and died making a hopeless gesture. Perhaps it is what we all should have done. For a warrior to skulk in the shadows until found probably went against all he believed in and so he did the only thing that he knew how to do. He died fighting for his King.

After this excitement the Danes hurriedly pushed all of their captives to the centre of the yard and, leaving us well guarded, made a slow and methodical search of the whole farm. We all stood together, shocked and demoralized, with our heads bowed and our minds reeling. All our struggle had come to nothing. We had now well and truly lost everything. Now that we had been captured we could not bring a new army to the aid of our people, could not return in force to smash the Danes. With the capture of the King all hope was gone.

To tell the truth I fully expected us to be killed at any moment. I had never heard of the Danes taking prisoners before and did not know what we should now expect. Were we to be returned to their camp for a life of slavery or were they just making sure that no one had escaped before they killed every man of us? I think all of us felt much the same. I tried to look around the group of captives for my father but turning my head sent stabbing jolts of pain down from my neck into my back. Each attempt brought tears to my eyes and I was forced to remain sitting where I was, in the mud, and staring straight ahead at the King.

I could make out little of Edmund's features for the torches were behind him and his face was cast in shadows. He sat opposite me, cross legged in the mud, and I could hear that he was praying quietly to himself. I was a little taken aback at this for I had never heard the King pray at any other time than in church. It was common enough for some of the men to mutter prayers, in fact some never seemed to stop, but Edmund had always seemed to be satisfied with his offerings in front of the priests. Now he prayed. It was not a prayer for his own safe deliverance, that much I could make out, but seemed to be for his kingdom as a whole. "Lord, from the fury of the Norsemen protect us". In the darkness and the mud, with my arms and back in agony, I quietly joined the King in his prayer.

We sat in the yard until near dawn and then, with the sky lightening to the east, we were all once again moved into the hall. Squatting and sitting against the walls it was still crowded within the small building for half a dozen Danes had joined us to act as our keepers. After a short while of edging nervously round us all they settled in much the same position as ourselves against the wall to either side of the door. A few small billets of wood had been thrown upon the fire and in the light from their glow I noticed the cauldron of oats that I had set by the fire the previous night. During the initial struggle it had been kicked over and I felt an odd sort of anger towards to man who had done it. With all the great things going on around me it was a spoiled meal that became the centre of my resentment. I suppose I was avoiding thinking of the larger problems by concentrating upon the smaller issues. Odd how the mind works.

I think I dozed a little as I squatted against the wall but even that was not easy for my hands were tied behind me and my neck throbbed continually. All of us were now silent and I found it difficult to estimate how much time passed. Drifting in and out of a doze and with the door closed it became hard to keep track of the hours.

When the door was finally opened again it was full light outside and we were led out into a day that had dawned clear, bright and chill. I realized from the position of the sun that it was already mid morning and that we had been locked up for over four hours. As each of us was led, bound and blinking, into the yard we were each taken hold of by a Danish warrior. When my turn came I was grabbed roughly by my bound hands, forcing my arms upwards, and I screamed out in pain. My captor, far from easing his hold, merely laughed and pulled my arms further up my back. I whimpered at the pain but told myself that I would not cry out again.

We were all led through the yard and out of the stockade's gateway in a long procession, two by two, captive and captor, and out onto the rough pasture that lay between the farm and a small wood. The pasture was crossed by two ruddy cart tracks and at the intersection stood a band of the enemy. That they were of high rank I did not doubt, for although dressed for war, their gear was all of a fine quality and they had the bearing of noblemen. We were led up in front of this group and there halted. Now I thought that our time on earth had ended and that we were about to be put to death in front of this small band of spectators. My fears were shared by several of the others for I could hear small prayers being muttered among my comrades. I had nothing to say. I felt merely a deep sense of frustration. I could have done so many things with my life had I only been given the chance. Now it was to be cut short merely to amuse a bunch of heathen onlookers. Under my breath I muttered curses not prayers.

A sharp kick to the back of my knees sent me tumbling to the ground and the jarring in my spine sent shoots of flame-bright pain into my mind. Lights flashed before my eyes and I felt as though I was about to vomit. I came to my senses again as the pain eased as I managed to haul myself into a kneeling position. Several of the others, older and less lithe, could not manage this and lay squirming face down on the turf. As I glanced to my side I saw that the only man still standing was the King. Edmund stood facing his adversaries with an iron stare. Gone was the dazed, mystical look of the previous day and in its place once again was the King I knew so well. Even travel stained and bound, caked in mud and, I noticed for the first time, dried oats, Edmund looked every inch the noble lord.

He was being addressed by one of the Danish leaders but so harsh was the man's accent that I found it difficult to understand what was being said. The few sections I could make out did not seem, at the time, to make much sense for they appeared to be asking Edmund if he would swear an oath to them.

I learnt later that they had actually offered Edmund his kingdom back in exchange for certain conditions. They wished for him to become a client king. A mere puppet of the Danish chiefs. A king who would pay them for the privilige of ruling his own land. They also wanted gold and lots of it.

It is obvious to me now that the Danes were more than a little afraid. They had come to England to secure a kingdom, which they had done in Northumbria, and had only really attacked the other kingdoms for the profit it might provide. They had no real wish to rule East Anglia and would rather it was done by Edmund. All they wanted was a heavy tax. Now they had suddenly found themselves faced with ruling two kingdoms separated by the powerful Mercians. They would fight us all if need be but would rather not have to do it quite yet.

The reply Edmund gave them was much easier to understand than the proposal. He simply stared at them and then spat at their feet. It was more than his pride, or any other man's pride, could bear to have his kingdom taken and then offered back as a bribe for betraying his own people. He would have none of it and showed them his contempt for even asking.

Well that one drop of spittle sealed his fate. Had he been a little less rash then perhaps he would still be alive today but his honour would not allow him to make a deal. On the day of my birth he had made an oath to his people to protect them and do his best to defend them. He had failed in his oath but was not about to add betrayal to his list of faults.

As the spit landed at the feet of the Danes I knew that Edmund was as good as dead. He knew it too for he laughed at the Danish leader's obvious rage and we all watched as his face went from pale anger to deep red fury. He strode forward and struck the King hard across the face with his axe shaft sending the King sprawling to the ground with blood fountaining from his nose. The Dane turned on his heel and stalked back to join his fellows shouting orders as he went.

We watched helplessly as the King was taken up and dragged off to the margin of the wood. Two of the warriors cut the bonds around his wrists and then refastened them behind a small oak tree. Edmund was now standing upright again, facing towards us. Several of our men cried out to him to make his peace but he would have none of it. I could see even through the blood and dirt that he was smiling at us. His face was already starting to swell where the ash shaft had struck him and he could obviously not talk but still he smiled at us. He knew what was going to happen. He knew he was going to die and he accepted it. Perhaps it was his way of paying the debt for all those he had sent to meet their deaths. Repaying their loyalty with his life. The two burly Danes then lay on with a mixture of fists and axe shafts.

Throughout the whole beating Edmund let forth not a sound. No cry came from his broken and smashed lips and although the pain must have been extreme he did not even groan. Enraged by this the Danes became more and more savage. I averted my eyes. I could bear to watch no more. The face that I had loved so well in life was now little more than a broken and bloody mask. I thanked God when Edmund finally passed out from the pain.

This was not good enough for the Danish leader for he ordered buckets of water to be brought from the farm and had Edmund doused until he again came round. When he was satisfied that the King was awake once more he grabbed a bow from one of his men and, carefully fitting the arrow, shot at the helpless Edmund. I watched in horror as the large Dane drew back the shaft, his face contorted into a terrible grin, as the arrow left the bow. It hit Edmund in the stomach. Not a killing wound, at least not to kill him quickly. The Dane had not wanted him to die straight away for he was already fitting a second shaft. This one hit him in the thigh.

After that I could watch no more. Tears streamed down my face and I yelled curses at the Danes at the top of my lungs. Many of the others were doing likewise and from the corner of my eye I made out my father weeping with the rest. Soon the rest of the Danes joined their commander and amongst our tears and curses could just be made out the sound of arrows striking home.

When the Danes left I do not know. I was locked into a small nightmarish world all of my own. My curses had been turned to screams when one of the Danes had kicked me in the small of the back and the lights appeared once more before my eyes. The second kick had caused me to mercifully pass out for the pain was so great. When I came to I felt sick and dizzy but was suprised to be alive at all.

I managed to glance around me and realised that the Danes had left. They had departed without even bothering to kill us. We had been left as living witnesses to the fate of our murdered King. I almost wished they had killed us too.

We all knelt or lay, desolate and angry, and swore revenge on the Danes. We were the lucky ones. We had lived through it all but none of us felt lucky. A small band of broken warriors, grieving and cursing while our hope lay broken, torn and bloody, pinned to an oak tree.

Pursuit and capture

It is at this point that the story becomes even more blurred and vague than it has been up until now.

Where did Edmund retreat to and where did he meet his death at the hands of the pursuing Danish army? The circumstances surrounding Edmund's capture, as related by his armour bearer via Abbo of Fleury, do seem to indicate that he was in retreat after the battle. Edmund had few troops with him and was in the open when caught by a larger force of Danes. The terms, mentioned by Abbo, offered to Edmund appear as those offered to a defeated monarch after battle.

Edmund was to remain in power as a subject king of the Danes but must surrender his **'Family treasures and inheritance'**. It is upon his refusal of these terms that he was made captive and executed.

The details of Edmund's death is one of the few things to have remained constant throughout the years and through all the retelling of the legend. According to Abbo of Fleury he was tied to a tree and lashed and when this did not break his spirit the Danes grew angry and started to shoot him with arrows. As if this was not enough they finally made an end of him by cutting off his head and throwing it into the forest.

If this story is based on truth then there may be more to the method of Edmund's martyrdom than appears on the surface. The almost ritual method of execution has direct parallels to the scourging and crucifixion of Christ and whether this was intended or not by the Danes, the early Saxon Church made full use of it. The removal of the head also has ritual significance in both Norse and pagan Saxon religions. The head was the vessel of the soul and a man who had lost his head would not be assured of his spirit passing to the next world. To cut off an enemy's head and remove it, so that they could not bury the body whole, was a calculated and direct insult to, not only the departed, but also his followers and family.

"Haegelisdun"

The honour, if such a word is suitable in these circumstances, to be regarded as the site of Edmund's martyrdom has been contested for by two separate villages- Hoxne in Suffolk and Hellesdon, near Norwich, in Norfolk. From the military point of view, and considering the circumstances surrounding the battle, both sites seem highly unlikely.

In Abbo of Fleury's account of Edmund's death the site of the martyrdom is named as 'Haegelisdun' and in a later account, written by Hermann of Bury in about 1095, the site of Edmund's martyrdom and initial burial is named as 'Suthtuna' or Sutton. These two names, 'Haegelisdun' and 'Sutton', are the only near contemporary clues that pinpoint the actual site of Edmund's death.

The traditional site of Edmund's death is Hoxne in Suffolk and although this tradition goes back many centuries it was not until well after the Norman conquest that it became established. In 950 the will of one bishop Theodred, a devotee of the Edmund cult, mentions Hoxne as having a church dedicated to St. Ethelbert [15] but no mention is made of Edmund.

The connection between Hoxne and the martyrdom are first made in 1101 by Bishop Herbert [16] of Norwich when in the foundation charter of his new cathedral at Norwich he refers to a chapel of St. Edmund at Hoxne. Bishop Herbert is also the first to mention that the chapel of St. Edmund as "where the martyr was killed".

Also, at about this time, the church at Hoxne was re-dedicated to Edmund and a small priory was created next to the chapel [17] in honour of the saint. These are the very earliest connections between Hoxne and Edmund. Although an unlikely site for the martyrdom Hoxne obviously had some very close connection with the cult of the saint a connection that has yet to be satisfactorily explained.

It has recently been suggested by Margaret Carey Evans in her book 'Hoxne and St. Edmund' that Archdeacon Hermanns 'Suthtuna' is a site in Hoxne. The only evidence presented to support the claim is that "there was and is in Hoxne parish a definite area called 'South-something'.

As a site for the martyrdom Hoxne is even less likely when viewed from a military perspective. For Edmund to reach Hoxne from the Thetford area would have involved travelling east along the Waveney valley. The area today is still marshy and prone to flooding and would have proved difficult terrain to a small fleeing group trying to move quickly.

We must also consider Edmund's destination. No help or support for the defeated king could be expected from the east. His army had been shattered and he had little chance of raising another with any speed. His best troops had been defeated and this is unlikely to have inspired confidence in a hastily raised second force. Edmund's main hope lay in reaching an ally who could afford him protection while he raised a new army.

Hellesdon, in Norfolk, seems just as unlikely as the site of the martyrdom as Hoxne. The only real point in its favour is its name, which in recent years has been suggested as a modern corruption of Abbo's 'Haegelisdun'.

Recent works, including those by Margaret Carey Evans, have had much to say upon the translation of 'Haegelisdun' to the modern 'Hellesdon' claiming that as a place name it will not translate satisfactorily. There can be no denying that it is insufficient to rely upon place name evidence that is at least 800 years old, but at least for Hellesdon there is some evidence. For Hoxne there is no evidence at all except the existence of a cult to the saint that can be proved not to have existed prior to the Norman conquest.

Apart from the connection with its name all other factors seem to point away from Hellesdon. To reach it Edmund would have to have travelled to the north. To do this would place himself in immediate danger. By travelling north he not only cut himself off from any potential help from Wessex but also allowed himself to become caught between the Danish army and the sea. If he went further to the north he ran the risk of meeting with other shipborne Danes upon the coast and becoming trapped between the two forces.

From a military standpoint Edmund's one logical escape route lay to the south. The Danes were coming from the west, the east and north afforded no protection and brought him nearer the coast. It was only from the south that support was likely to be forthcoming.

It is to the south, and the Stour river crossings at Bures and Glemsford that would see him safely in the lands controlled by the kingdom of Wessex. It is to Wessex that the Mercians had looked for aid two years previously, and where Edmund could now find troops with which to regain his kingdom. The route south was open to him whereas the other routes only led him into more danger.

To head to the north or east not only placed him in danger but also involved travelling over rough country. The route south lay straight and clear down the old Roman road from the river crossing at Knettishall, a mere four miles to the east of Thetford. If the battle had taken place at the eastern river crossing from there the road through Suffolk would have stretched before him.

In heading south Edmund had a fast escape route and furthermore he could rely on the remains of his fleeing army to cause confusion as they were pursued around the Thetford area. The possibility of Edmund being able to raise a new East Anglia force, with any speed, was slim. His best troops had been defeated and he would have to gather more local militia troops who would already be aware that a better force than themselves had failed. To head south was the logical action for the defeated king to take. Wessex was an ally with a potentially large army. To combine his troops with the West Saxons might not have been enough to defeat the Danes but it may have forced a peace, as it did at Nottingham, and compelled the Danes to retire once more to York.

For the Danes to have pursued Edmund south of the Stour would have meant fighting the army of Wessex, not from behind earthworks, as at Nottingham, but in the open and shortly after fighting a major battle against Edmund. Wessex could be left for the next campaigning season.

127

The other 'Haegilisdun'

In recent years a new possible site for the martyrdom has come to light that not only ties in with the theory that Edmund retreated to the south but also supports the proposition of Edmund using the Roman road.

In 1978 Stanley West, a Suffolk archaeologist, was studying tithe maps dating to 1840 for the area around Bradfield St. Clare in Suffolk. Just to the south of Pritchers Green was a field called 'Hellesden'. A mile to the south, on the parish boundary between Cockfield and Bradfield Combust, he noticed a place called Sutton Hall. He further noticed that to the north, in the parish of Rougham, are Kingshall farm, street and green. This not only brought together both Sutton and Haegelisdun but placed them near a possible royal residence and all lie in a parrallel line within a mile of the Roman road.

If this is the site of the martyrdom it does go some way to explaining not only the directly contradictory evidence of Abbo and Hermann but also the reason behind Edmund's interment at Bury. If he had died near Norwich why would he not be buried there, or even at the Saxon cathedral at North Elmham? If he died at Hoxne why would his remains be carried to Bury when it was as easy to carry them to the larger settlements of Norwich, Thetford or even the old bishops see at Dunwich?

To accept that the Bradfield site is the place of the martyrdom means that the two earliest references of Abbo and Hermann do not contradict each other but do in fact support each other. The Bradfield site not only fits all the place name evidence but also fits with the tradition of the battle having been fought near Thetford. It must be regarded as the only site which fits the military, literary and traditional evidence.

The obvious reason for the remains of the sainted king to be placed at Bury was because it was the nearest large religious settlement to the original shrine at Sutton. All three sites, Hellesden, Sutton and Kingshall, are within five miles of Bury St Edmunds. The site at Bradfield St. Clare would appear to be the strongest contender for the site of the martyrdom of East Anglia's saintly king.

The Witness

You ask me now "What of the saint?". Well I have told you all I can tell you. Perhaps he was a saint. It is so long ago now that I cannot tell.

I have told you what I remember though and if that is not good enough then I suggest you go and talk to the monks. For me he was a King. A King first and a kind man second. He cared for those around him, liked all those he could and was kind to many. He tried his best to defend his people and that he lost it all was no fault of his own. If those things are what makes a saint then saint he was.

Listen now. Listen to an old man. Edmund was flesh and blood much the same as you or I. Whatever the monks and priests tell you that is the one thing they can never deny. He was born, he loved, he ate bread and drank ale and then he was killed. I saw no wondrous miracles. I saw no signs from God. But perhaps those signs only come to those who are worthy of them or want to see them. I knew a King. That is the truth. If you do not care for my tale then go and listen to the priests. Perhaps their tale will be more to your liking.

But whichever tale you do choose to listen to remember this. That both tales are but stories. Stories told because they have meaning for both sides that tell them. For me it is to perhaps bring back the days of my youth. To return to a happier time. A time before the Danes. The priests also have a reason for telling their story. No I cannot tell you what it is but be assured they do have their reasons. But above all remember that both are just stories. The real King Edmund, the real saint Edmund is probably a mystery to both of us.

The one thing we all have in common are the bones. If they belonged to a saint I do not know. Perhaps that is for none of us to decide.

Now you tire me with all your questions. I am too old for such worries. If you still want answers then I can only suggest that you go down into the church and seek them yourself. I have done enough, so go away now and leave my old bones to rest in peace.

Close the door on the way out. It gets so cold in here. So very cold.

From Boedericsworth to Bury

With Edmund's death many of the early chronicles really begin. The story relates that his body was left lying where it fell while his head was thrown into the woods. When his followers arrived they could find no trace of the head and a search was organized. While searching the deepest thicket they heard a voice shouting "Here, here, here" and on following the shouts found the head of the King lying between the paws of an enormous wolf. It was the severed head that had called to them and upon placing it back on the neck it miraculously rejoined itself.

The loyal followers coffined the newly restored body in a decent manner and carried it to the nearby village of Sutton. Here they erected a makeshift shelter and placed the coffin within. Here, according to Abbo, the body of St. Edmund remained for many years.

The actual date that the translation of the Saint's bones took place is unclear but at some point in the century after his death Edmund's remains were moved from their makeshift shrine at Sutton to a new shrine at Boedericsworth [later Bury St Edmunds]. Once at Bury the miracles attributed to the saint multiplied and the shrine became one of the most visited in England. Kings and nobles joined with peasants and craftsmen in their wish to pay homage to the martyred King and the revenues of the shrine grew very great.

The shrine was given into the hands of twenty secular canons until 1020 when Bishop Ailwin granted the shrine and community of St. Edmund free from episcopal control and substituted twenty monks from the Benedictine house of St Benet's and from Ely.

After the Norman conquest great building works took place at Bury until Bury St. Edmunds abbey and church were agreed to be amongst the finest and richest in all England. Although the abbey suffered from the ravages of both fire and civil disturbance [one notable case in 1327 combining the two] it carried on as a monastic institution until the dissolution of the monastaries by Henry VIII in 1539.

It would be pleasing to say at this point that the bones of the saint rested peacefully at Bury throughout this period. Unfortunately, this is not the case.

The location of the bones of St. Edmund are now as great a mystery as the site of his martyrdom ever was. It is claimed by some that they were stolen by the French during the reign of King John and others claim that they are now in the Howard family chapel at Arundel castle. Others claim that the bones of the saint perished along with the shrine at the time of the dissolution. What ever the truth is, and that we may never know, it may be hoped that the bones of the Anglo-Saxon king and saint rest in peace.

NOTES UPON THE TEXT

1. King Offa - King of Mercia 757 - 796

2. Dating as in the Anglo-Saxon Chronicle [ASC] : A. Savage 1995

3. Throughout the text I refer to 'Danes' to cover a variety of peoples. The Anglo-Saxons referred to the invaders as Danes, Vikings, Heathens and Pagans. Although many of the invaders did originate in Denmark it is not being used as a geographical term.

4. ASC. A. Savage 1995

5. Alcuin of York. Pupil of Egbert, Archbishop of York. Summoned by Charles the Great in 782 to organize the palace school in Gaul.

6. ASC. A. Savage 1995

7. The Anglo-Saxons. D. Wilson 1971

8. Medieval Foundation of England. G. O. Sayles 1948

9. The Anglo-Saxons. D. Wilson 1971

10. The Black Fens. A. K. Astbury

11. Seven Viking Romances. Palsson & Edwards

12. 'The Battle of Maldon' was written shortly after the battle which took place in 991 A.D.

13. Orderic Vitalis - Born in Shropshire and became a monk at St. Evroul in Normandy. He wrote an account of England and Normandy between 1123 and 1141.

14. Bishop Humbert - Traditionally Bishop during the reign of King Edmund.

15. St Ethelbert - Probably not the more famous Ethelbert of Kent but Ethelbert of East Anglia. Murdered at Sutton Wells in Herefordshire for dynastic reasons, a considerable cult grew up around him. Hereford cathedral is dedicated to St. Ethelbert and St. Mary.

16. Herbert de Losinga - Founder of Norwich cathedral in 1095. Probably born in Suffolk in the parish of Syleham at Monk's Hall. Curiously this is the next parish to Hoxne and, therefore, Herbert's belief that Hoxne was the site of the martyrdom need be no more than a 'local' tradition [Spurden, Norfolk Archaeology Vol 111]. Spurden goes on to say "Bishop Herbert was not Norman by birth, but an Englishman, born at his father's manor at Syleham, in the hundred of Hoxne in the county of Suffolk". Herbert died in 1119 after having held the bishopric for 29 years.

17. The priory at Hoxne was established by charter about the year 1116, yet was not completed and consecrated until 1267.

BIBLIOGRAPHY

Anglo-Saxon England : B.B.C publications 1957

Anglo-Saxon Chronicle : G.N.Garmonsway - Everyman Library 1953

Anglo-Saxon Chronicle : A. Savage - Tiger Books 1995

Anlo-Saxon Thegn [The] : M.Harrison & G.Embleton - Osprey 1993

Anglo-Saxons [The] : D.Wilson - Penguin 1971

Black Fens [The] ; A.K.Astbury - Providence Press 1987

British Museum Guide to Anglo-Saxon Antiquities 1923 : R.A.Smith - Anglia Publishing 1993

Byrhtnoth, Anglo-Saxon Warrior : J.McSween - Ely Cathedral 1991

Chronicle of the Abbey of Bury St Edmunds : Joscelin of Brakeland - Translated D.Greenaway & J.Sayer - Oxford University Press 1989

Corolla Sancti Edmundi : Lord Francis Hervey - 1907

Dictionary of **Saints** : Donald Attwater - Penguin 1965

Doomsday Book/Norfolk : Phillipa Brown - Phillimore 1984

History of Roman Britain : P.Salway - O.U.P 1993

Hoxne and St Edmund : Margaret Carey Evans - B.C.Publications 1995

In Search of the Dark Ages : M.Wood - 1981

Medieval Foundations of England : G.O.Sayles - Methuen 1948

New Site for the Martyrdom of St Edmund : S.E.A.West - Suffolk Arch. No. 35 ,1983

St Edmund, King and Martyr : Bryan Houghton - Terence Dalton 1970

Seven Viking Romances : H.Polsson & P.Edwards - Penguin 1985

Vikings [The] : I.Heath & A.McBride - Osprey 1985

Wanderings in Anglo-Saxon Britain : A.Weigall - Hodder & Stoughton